Mixed Emotions

(NOT)NORMAL

KATY HUNTER

(Not)Normal

ISBN # 978-1-83943-792-2

©Copyright Katy Hunter 2022

Cover Art by Erin Dameron-Hill ©Copyright April 2022

Interior text design by Claire Siemaszkiewicz

Totally Bound Publishing

(NOT)NORMAL

Dedication

To all the people who feel like a square peg in a round hole. May you find your way.

Acknowledgements

I would like to thank everybody at Totally Bound, especially Jamie Rose, my editor. Thank you to my WB sisters who are always there for me and to Rosanna, Sara, Lauriel and all my other author friends, for making me laugh and keeping me on track.

Prologue

Milly

"So I told him…goodbyyyyye!"

I keep the last note going as long as I can, but it wavers a little toward the end. A warm-up might have been a good idea, since my voice is seriously out of practice. Yesterday's rehearsal was the first time I've sung on stage since God knows when. The crowd erupts, and I thank my lucky stars that this has been a success. This gig is brimming with A-list performers and I'm a has-been — C-list at the very most.

"Milly! Milly! Milly!" roars the crowd, wanting more.

"Thank you! Thank you so much!" I point at the crowd. I'm nothing without them.

There's no reason for any of the people out there to be cheering so loudly. But they love it. Maybe it's nostalgia, or I've just lucked out and a few of my old fans are in the crowd. Whatever it is, it's exhilarating.

I'm on a high that it's going to be difficult to come down from.

For a second I want to go back. My brain wipes away the bad memories, and I forget about how much I hate touring and management and the invasion of my privacy. I want to stay up on this stage forever, absorb all this positive emotion, sing the songs that I love.

The lights come up and I thank the audience then my honorary musicians. They offered to come along and play today out of the kindness of their hearts. Anything for a good cause. They are a mix of guys I've worked with in the past and a couple of friends of friends. They're good people.

What if I hired them, wrote some songs, went on a short tour? *Nothing* beats this feeling.

The call to do such an impressive charity show was a surprise. I'd given up everything to go off to college for a couple of years, finish my education, but I take the occasional gig here and there. I never made as much money as everybody thinks I did—just enough to get by and some savings put aside for traveling. I'm not poor, but my bank account can always do with topping up.

"Thank you, Milly," says Zane, the compere for the evening. He walks out onto the stage and over to me, grabbing my arm to keep me here. "A little birdy tells me that you recently finished college and that you're about to do some traveling."

Uh-huh. I nod, nervously. *Where's he going with this?* I don't exactly talk about my private life, especially now. I'm not *'Milly the celebrity'* anymore. I gave that up.

"Yeah," I reply. "And?"

"Well, this little birdy told me that he wants to come, too." *Zane wants to travel with me?*

Oh, no. No, no, make it stop. He's pointing off to the side of the stage where my boyfriend, or rather future *ex*-boyfriend, is striding into the spotlight.

My stomach sinks and I kind of want it to pull me down and under the stage. I glance down at my feet. *Trap doors. Do they still have them? Nope, apparently not.* Zane's hand is still firmly gripping my arm, stopping me from going anywhere. This is great publicity for their show. These days it's not enough to have amazing singers. You've got to have a little gossip and scandal, too. I'm about to give them the latter.

"No." I grit my teeth and turn to Zane, still smiling. If the million phone cameras pointed at me right now are any good, they have to be capturing the sheer horror in my eyes. That'll be online before you can blink.

My boyfriend, beautiful as he is, is about to discover rejection in front of all these people, and he has only himself to blame. I wrench my arm from Zane's grip and stroll over toward him. The grin on my about-to-be-ex's face is priceless. He must think he's *so* clever, doing this here. However this ends — as he well knows — this is going to give him that much-sought-for step up into the limelight.

"Don't do it," I say through my gritted smile.

He lifts a microphone to his mouth, drops to one knee and holds out a ring.

Fuck.

I block out everything — the sound of the crowd, the roadies crouching down beside and around me trying to empty the stage without getting in the way. I block out Zane as he does some kind of running commentary. I ignore the man at my feet.

Funnily enough, the hardest thing to shut out is the voice in the back of my mind that keeps repeating, *If you say no, Mum's going to kill you.* She's watching this right now. My whole family is. In fact, if I wasn't trying to block it out, too, I'd know this from the fact that I can hear her ringtone coming from my back pocket as I try so hard to make myself disappear.

He begins to speak and the crowd hushes. "Milly. I've known you for less than a year, but when you find the love of your life, you just know." *If you knew anything after 'less than a year' then you'd know that this is a terrible, awful idea.* "I love you and I want to spend the rest of my life with you."

I close my eyes and breathe in and out. Trying to make myself disappear didn't work. I'm still here. The earth didn't swallow me up. I did not float away. I am going to have to deal with this in the only way I can. It's not going to be pretty.

I step forward, clasp the ring, the box, his hand and push it toward him. "No," I say, only loud enough for him to hear. "I told you that I didn't want a wedding or babies or forever. You knew this."

"You... You don't love me?"

I shake my head. "No."

"You don't want to marry me? But...I love you."

"No." Anger swells inside me and it takes all I've got not to shove him off this stupid stage. *How dare you do this to me?* "Fuck off, just *fuck off!*"

He face forms this sort of vengeful, hurt scowl. "You were just using me for my body."

Yes. Have you seen your body? Of course I was. Well, that's not entirely true. I enjoyed his company, somewhat, and we had fun. Not 'get married and have babies' fun, but it wasn't *that* casual.

"Yes?" I reply, not wanting to go into the details.

A collective gasp comes from the crowd. The microphone is picking up everything I'm saying. *Oh,*

God. I scan the audience, trying to find at least one person nodding and giving me a thumbs-up.

Somebody out there gets this, right? They get that I don't want this, that there's nothing wrong with me for saying no, for being so shocked at the damned cheek of such an intimate, unwarranted, undesired moment being shared with the whole damn world.

Especially when he *knew* I'd say no. How can he think that I'd say yes? I made myself very, *very* clear.

Argh. I'm faced with a crowd of romantics, their hearts breaking into collective pieces in empathy with the man in front of me. He drops his head, followed by his hand, the ring box tumbling to the ground. His second knee sinks to the ground, and he folds up into a big, bawling pile of sad.

Shit. I can't do this. I turn, but Zane is heading for me, so I turn back and leap over my now-ex, who is prostrate on the floor. The crowd does a collective *'what-the-fuck?'* sound.

Did I really just jump over the man I turned down? Yes. Yes, I did.

I take one last look back at the mess I've left on stage and I run away, past the people offstage, their expressions as gobsmacked as the audience. I run to my trailer, grab my stuff, ignoring my manager who tries to block my exit, screaming things at me about *'responsibility'* and *'pleasing the public'*. I run out of there, out of the VIP area, past the crowds, the marketing stands and straight to the car park.

Out of breath and out of my mind, I rip open my car door and throw myself and my stuff into the car. I lock the doors and drive myself out of that place as quickly as the exiting traffic will allow. Only when I'm gone, when I can pull over, do I stop and breathe and cry huge, racking sobs as I'm slumped over the steering wheel.

I should never have come back. This is not my life anymore. I have things to do with my life that don't include any of these people. I need to get away. I need to be alone.

I get it. I'm not normal. I'm not like them.

Chapter One

Milly

Sal taps on the steering wheel to the beat of the country music blasting out of the radio. The windows are wound down to the max, and the tires are speeding along the road a little fast for my liking.

"Is it far?" I'd quite like it not to be far. My legs are sticking to the fake leather seats. *That's going to pinch.*

"No. Twenty minutes or so."

It's already been twenty-five minutes. How big is this place? Ever since we left Austin, all I've seen is the occasional red barn or auto shop and one or two shooting ranges. Otherwise, it's flat, dry countryside as far as the eye can see.

I'm about to discover my new normal.

Normal. I hate that word. It packs people up in neat little boxes. My mum likes to use it when referring to anybody who isn't *exactly* like her.

Me, for example.

"*It's not normal, Milly.*" She'd brought it out when I'd run off at sixteen to be a popstar, when I'd given that up to go to college and *again* when I'd refused to bring any boyfriends home, because, well, none of them were going to last long enough for her to get attached. She might have brought it up once or twice when a video of me breaking my ex-boyfriend's heart went viral. Then this... Flying across the world to Austin to help Sal run her coffee shop. Carrie is sick, like really sick, and Sal needs help.

And I *really* need to get away.

Mum thinks people should stay in one place. She's always lived in the town she grew up in. She met and married my dad there, bought a home there. It's like she got everything she needed with two minutes' walk of the town center, cemented her feet to the floor and never moved again.

I will *never* cement my feet anywhere. You can quote me on that.

I can't think of anything worse. How can you not want to see the world? Experience all the things? Taste all those delicious mouths that are just waiting to be kissed?

I've seen what marriage does to people, how it numbs their sense of adventure. I want to *feel*.

"Do you have to go in today?" I ask.

She turns to me and smiles, looking exactly like my dad for a split second. Luckily for her, that's one of the very few things they have in common. "No, honey, you've got me all to yourself until tomorrow. Carrie's got it covered." Carrie is Sal's '*close friend*'. I'm pretty sure she's a lot more than that, but Sal has never been one to share things like that with our side of the family. I guess I'll find out soon enough.

"And when do I start?" I lean down and grab my bag. Thinking about Carrie reminds me that I should call Mum and Dad, tell them I got here okay. I fiddle with my phone while Sal explains how the shift system works.

"So, it's basically part-time. You start straight away, but we'll ease you in." Good. I'm no barista. Sal's coffee shop is supposedly the best in town, and I'm not ready for that kind of responsibility yet.

Sal packed her bags at eighteen and ran away to America in search of Melrose Place. I don't know where that is, but she told my dad that it had to be better than home. She met Carrie shortly afterward and they moved to a little town a few miles out of Austin, set up their business and never looked back.

I've never quite worked out how moving across the world, settling down and working in the same place for your whole life is any different from what she would have done had she stayed at home, but I guess it's warmer—a *lot* warmer. The trails of sweat trickling down my back right now can attest to this fact.

Eventually, love makes everybody cement their feet to the floor.

I twist and turn the ancient buttons in front of me. One of them falls off into my hand. "Doesn't this car have air conditioning?"

She chuckles. "The air conditioning hasn't worked on this old thing for years. I keep telling Carrie we need to get a new car but *goddammit* that woman loves her Pontiac more than me."

Unbuttoning my blouse in an attempt to get some kind of respite, I lean out of the window, letting my arm catch the gusts of wind as we race on down the road. Being blasted by hot air is slightly more pleasant than wallowing in it.

Precisely seventeen minutes later we draw up in front of their beautiful home. Admittedly you have to drive down the bumpiest, dustiest lane to get there, but it's totally worth losing all the feeling in your bum.

"Her grandmother left her the land, and we built on it. Six acres." Sal grabs my suitcase from the boot of the car and stands beside me, admiring her massive house.

Sal and Carrie have the kind of place that I could only ever dream of owning. It's a mansion compared to what I left behind. Back home, houses are small and stuck together. If you strike lucky, you get an end of terrace with an alleyway that goes down the side. This place has a front porch, a double garage and a garden five times bigger than itself.

I'm not jealous. There's nothing more stifling than buying a house. But if I did want one, it would probably need to look like this.

"And she doesn't mind me staying?" I have fond memories of the few times I've met her. She would play board games with me when I was little and take me to the park, but I don't know a lot about Carrie from an adult's point of view, other than the fact that she is my aunt's partner.

"Are you joking? You're the daughter we never had. Prepare to be smothered." I haven't been filled in on the intricacies of Carrie's illness, but I know it's bad. Bad enough for my dad to shed a tear, and he never cries. Another member of the household is going to be a burden on the two of them, no matter how much they love me.

I grab my auntie and pull her in for a spontaneous hug. The woman is skin and bones. She works too hard and, as I'm beginning to understand, worries too hard, too. "I missed you, Auntie Sally. Can we go see Carrie right now? I need more hugs." Carrie is the opposite of

Sal. She's all boobs and bum. The two of them are polar opposites, and yet it works. It has for twenty-five years.

We drag my suitcase into the front hall.

"Do you want a glass of water or something?" Bright, modern paintings adorn every wall, interspersed with landscapes and portraits. The house is open plan, light and bright—and hospital-level clean. There is not a speck of dust in the place.

Are they really going to want me living here? I'm twenty-one on the outside, but those who have had the misfortune to share a house with me might suggest that I stopped maturing at around age seventeen.

I gulp down my water as we close up the house and head off to the coffee shop, and I place the pristine crystal glass on a side-table by the front door as we leave. My disruption to their perfect home has begun, and it's only the first day.

I'm more than exhausted but too excited to sleep. Leaning in to check myself in the car's side-view mirror, I'm horrified by what I see before me. There are bags under my eyes big enough to have paid the extra baggage allowance. I look too much like I've been on a packed plane for fourteen of the last sixteen hours. Then again, when did I ever look fancy?

* * * *

"Honey, you are a sight for sore eyes. Come over here and give your Aunt Carrie a hug." She doesn't look ill. Maybe a few pounds lighter but she's chirpy enough. She's brought so much vivacity into the precious few moments I've spent in her presence that I've never forgotten her—especially that crowning glory of hair forming a perfect halo of curls around her face.

Her arms are outstretched, reminding me, too, that this woman hasn't worn a bra in her whole damn life — or at least every time I've seen her.

"That isn't normal," my mum would say behind Aunt Carrie's back. I was never quite sure if she was referring to the lack of underwear or the fact that Dad's sister was essentially married to a woman. Both of those things made Mum's lips tighten with concern. Another thing to add to the list of opinions that I do *not* share with my own mother.

I barrel into those arms and snuggle into her chest as she hugs me tight. "I missed you, too." Carrie and Sal get me. They understand why I didn't want to marry the boy next door, and they get my need for adventure.

We sit at the counter on high stools with padded backs on them. They swivel like office chairs, much to my amusement. The coffee shop is way more modern that I imagined, with wooden counters and industrial pipes. They have one of those enormous blackboards going along the back wall with every coffee combination you could wish for on it. The picture in my mind of a clichéd fifties diner is far from reality. They serve me apple pie and an ice-cold milkshake, which is much more in line with my preconceived ideas.

I stretch the ache of traveling out of my shoulders. The shop is the first place since I got here with any kind of regulated temperature, and it's glorious. I may just stay right here on this stool for the next year, breathing in the cold, welcome air.

The jingle of the door reveals a smartly dressed old man. He trundles in, tips his hat at us. "Afternoon, Harry," says Sal, popping behind the counter. "The usual?"

He sits in a window table, takes off his hat — placing it carefully on the tabletop — and grins widely at Sal. "Please."

"This is Harry, one of our best customers," says Carrie, winking at him. "In the summer he has a sweet tea and a slice of pie." Sal slides the tray toward me, and I take it over. Looks like she's got me working already.

"You the new girl?" asks Harry. His smile reveals hardly any teeth. I guess he's been drinking sweet tea for a while now.

"She's my niece," replies Sal. "She's come all the way from England just to serve you, Harry. She a singer, you know…famous back home." I clench my jaw. I guess I'm not going to get away without anybody mentioning it.

He chuckles and holds up his glass. "Welcome. It'll be sweeter on my ears to hear someone singing along to the radio in *tune* for once."

"You'd do well to remember who makes you your pie every day," says Carrie, huffing in fake annoyance. You can sense the homeliness in this place. I didn't expect any less from the aunties. They're big old softies. With any luck, it'll make it easier to fit in. Small communities like this tend to be tight knit, and I'm not exactly everybody's cup of tea.

The door jingles again and this time it's a middle-aged woman. She appears to be melting from the sweltering heat, sweat dripping from every pore. "Delivery, ladies." Carrie and Sal head to the back of the shop to bring in the boxes and I move around to behind the counter.

"What do you think, Harry? Do I look like I know what I'm doing?" He nods and laughs.

"Sure do. Any chance of a refill?" He holds up his glass and I look around for the pitcher of iced tea. "In the 'frigerator behind you," he adds, helpfully.

I bend down to grab it and the door jingles again. That's going to get really annoying really quickly. Whirling around, pitcher in hand, I come face to face with a handsome cowboy. It's the Stetson and the plaid shirt that seals the deal, but the sapphire-blue eyes and blond stubble on that perfectly square jaw don't hurt, either.

I'd packed up and left home so quickly when Sal had called two days before that it hadn't even occurred to me that there would be cowboys here. Handsome cowboys, at that.

"Hi!" I say, flashing my best customer-service smile. "Just a second and I'll be with you." I pop around the counter and serve Harry his drink then give my full attention to my gorgeous new customer. Fingers crossed *he's* a regular too. "How can I help you?"

He looks me up and down, blushes, stuttering out the quietest words. "Is Sal here?"

"She's in the back." The cowboy smiles nervously, shakes his head and backs out of the store. I turn to Harry. "Was it something I said?"

"More like something you wore." Harry stares up at my chest.

Crap. My hands fling to cover my breasts. My blouse is unbuttoned down to my navel from when I was in the car. I've been showing a considerable amount of British boob since I got here. No wonder Harry has such a big grin on his face. I throw him a look, and he has the decency to bow his head.

"Oh my God." Sal and Carrie walk back through. "Why didn't you tell me I had my boobs out for the lads?" I ask, my teeth gritted, turning around and buttoning myself back up. This was *not* how I'd intended to start my life here.

"I didn't even notice," says Sal, placing a comforting hand on my shoulder and giving it a squeeze. "I'm sure nobody saw."

"I scared away one of your customers."

Carrie's eyes widen. "Who?"

"One of the Booth boys—Evan, I think," answers Harry.

Jaws drop and Sal and Carrie share an *'oh shit'* look. "What's so bad?" I ask. "Who are they?" *Have I fucked up already?*

"The Booths pretty much own this town. They're spread out far and wide, seven kids in the last generation, each of them with several of their own now. Evan is the third oldest of the middle child, Mark. They're like royalty around here." Considering how she's describing them, her voice lacks any respect.

I bite my lip. "I didn't mean to—"

"No, you didn't," interrupts Carrie. "And they're used to us, anyway. It's not as if Sal and I are their favorite people, either. I grew up here, so we're tolerated. You're my niece, as far as I'm concerned, so you belong here, too. I'm sure it'll be fine." She pulls me in for a reassuring side-hug.

"We'll apologize on Sunday." Sal grins at me. "Once a month we're invited to the Booth family home for buffet and grill."

"Lunch at the royal palace? I'm going to need a new dress."

Sal looks me up and down, squinting at my jean shorts. "You're not wrong, actually. We're going to need to cover you up a little. People are a little more... conservative over here."

Cover up? In this heat? I thought we'd be stripping off. Looks like my new normal is going to be something else entirely.

Chapter Two

Milly

I pull at my preppy summer dress. The high collar is not something I'm used to, and I'm choking in here. "Stop fussing. People here have certain standards. You'll get used to it, but it's not like home," says Sal.

You can say that again. On my first night Carrie sat me down and asked me to dress appropriately and to follow their lead in public. *What does that even mean? Who are these people that I can't be myself around them?*

This strait-jacket version of a dress is not what my body is accustomed to at all. My legs are hidden under a thick cotton skirt and my breasts and shoulders are wondering what they did so terribly wrong to be restrained in such a way. I'm doing this for my aunties — and only my aunties.

Carrie isn't coming with us. She has slept every day since I got here, poor love. Today will be no different.

I, however, have been working my butt off. After three days of intense training with Sal, my coffee no longer tastes like dirty dishwater—or so she says. She might just be being nice. My lattes are still lacking and my sweet iced tea? Well, it's iced. One out of two isn't bad, right?

"I'm really not sure this is my thing, Auntie." I never signed up for *Little House on the* fucking *Prairie.*

"The dress or the party?" She scrunches up her nose, like she gets it—but I still have to go.

"Both." The people here seem friendly enough, but Sal's right. They're different from back home. It's like I've been flung back to a cute little black-and-white movie from 1952. Everybody's super courteous and polite. Nobody swears or mucks around. It's all a little too perfect for me. Eerie, even.

And hot. Why does it have to be so fucking hot? I'm already sweating like a pig in a blanket and probably look like one, too.

At least I'm not sticking to the seat this time, so there's that. I lean out of the window to get a better look at the house we're parking in front of. The Booth mansion is even bigger than Sal's place—gaudier, flashier, too. In case you were in any doubt about who was the boss around here, they've made it perfectly clear with Roman columns, a couple of impressive marble lions and a touch of gold.

People are getting out of their cars, oven dishes in their hands, and walking around the house to the garden. The faces here are beginning to feel familiar. Susan, for example, comes into the coffee shop almost every day, sits at the back and smokes one of those electronic cigarettes. She never buys anything, and I'm never allowed to ask why.

She's accompanied by her husband today. He is without a doubt a member of the Booth family. There must be a factory somewhere just outside of the village where they make a couple of Booths a year. They've never bothered to change the mold. Susan looks over at me and Sal and smiles. Sal squeezes my elbow, but I'm not ignorant. I get it. I'm hardly going to run over and blurt out that she spends half her life in our little café.

Out the back of the house, the garden — or yard, as they call it here — is beautiful. Flowers are in bloom, and chairs and tables are set out for the guests. This Booth is mayor or sheriff or something. I lost interest when Carrie tried to tell me the Booth family tree.

Evan is there, hanging out with several other clones — brothers or cousins, perhaps. The Booth gene is strong. They are accompanied by a group of girls who are dressed like me but look as though they like it. Not a single woman is wearing trousers or jeans, and none of the women under forty have short hair.

Mine is long-ish and pink — and has odd sticky-out bits from a photoshoot a couple of months ago. They were going for punk. It looked great for five minutes, but now it's more like a Miley Cyrus' mullet on a bad day. I lift my hand to my head in an attempt to make it…what? Prettier, maybe? Less pink? It's silly and I know it, but I'm here for the long haul, and I need to fit in for the time it takes Carrie to get better.

"I like it," a voice whispers into my ear.

"Sorry?" I spin on my heels and find myself face to face with Evan's twin. My breath hitches. There's a hot cowboy two inches away from my nose and for a few seconds longer than is acceptable with a stranger. We lock eyes.

"No need to apologize. Your hair. It's different. I like it. You must be Milly Parker, the coffee shop girl." He smiles at me and takes a step back so we're not breathing on each other's faces, using the opportunity to check out my highly unflattering dress.

Oh my God. The coffee shop girl. Not *'the singer'* or *'that girl from that video'*. I've never been so relieved to be described as just *'the coffee shop girl'*.

"I wasn't apologizing, and yes, I like it, too. Needs a trim, though. And you are?" I hold out a hand to shake.

"Eli. Elijah Booth. I'm Evan's older brother. You met him the other day in the coffee shop." He doesn't shake my hand, so I just stand there, my arm out, wondering if he knows about me flashing my boobs at his brother. There's no smirk, no wink-wink-nudge-nudge. Maybe Evan kept his story to himself. "I'm being rude. Shall we get you something to drink? Then I'll introduce you to everybody."

With a cup of sweet tea in hand, I follow Eli over to the others. His impeccable composure unnerves me. He is completely unfazed by my presence, like he meets pink-haired British girls every day. This is *not* the case for the rest of the group.

They are fascinated by me — way overly friendly for people I just met. I'm bombarded with a million questions about England and the Queen. I don't know why I thought they would judge me for my hair. That's the last thing that interests them.

The women in the group huddle together a couple of feet away from the men. None of them are coupled up. We're like eight-year-olds on the playground. Boys are icky and to be tolerated at arm's length. And yet, from all appearances, not a one of them is under eighteen.

"Is it true," asks Mackenzie, "that you're famous? My uncle Harry said that Sal says you're famous." The attention around me goes up a notch, and I step back away from them to breathe.

"Yes. Well, yes and no. I won a competition when I was sixteen. It was on TV, *Star-Factor*. I got a recording contract and brought out a couple of songs. Then I went to college, and I've just been writing since then, doing the odd gig or interview here and there. I haven't actually recorded anything in three years."

"Sing something," says a male voice from a few feet away. It's Eli. *Of course it is.* Does he not believe me? I suppose I don't look very famous. And nobody here would have heard of me.

I grab my phone and google myself. Been a while since I did that. I scroll past *that* video, looking up and around to make sure none of them saw. My second song was a love song, not too shocking for this crowd. I hit play and their eyes light up, sending tingles down my spine. The thrill of sharing my music will never die. I switch it off and steer the conversation away from myself. I didn't come here to be *famous-me*, I came here to be *family-me*.

"Are y'all coming to The Clearing with us later?" asks Raylyn. She spells her name with two Ys. Everybody spells it with at least one 'I', but, she informed me with a giggle, two Ys is so much easier to remember.

"Oh, you have to come," adds Mackenzie. We never shorten it to Mack...or Kenzie, I'm told. I strive to remember all their names, but I know I'm going to forget at least half of them.

My glance is drawn to Eli, who is in deep conversation with a brown-haired boy whose name has already evaporated from my mind. "Is everybody going?"

"I think so," she replies.

I flash them a smile. "Well then, yes, I'd love to. What's 'The Clearing', though?"

"Oh, just a nice place to hang out." Raylyn with two Ys giggles with delight. "You'll see."

Everybody over here drives, so there's a friendly battle for who's taking whose car. No need for a designated driver here. I haven't seen a single person take a sip of alcohol since I got into town.

"That's not normal," I mutter under my breath. *Ugh,* I sound like my mother. It's not, though. A glass of chilled Californian chardonnay or a cool beer would have been very welcome on arrival, but everybody in this town loves their tea, sweetened to within an inch of its life. How they all have such radiant smiles, I have no idea. The dentists here must work overtime.

* * * *

Eli

"Jesus, Evan, you kept that one to yourself." When he came running into the house the other day hollering about a new girl in the café and that she was showing off her bra *"like them ladies we saw in Houston that time"*, he hadn't mentioned that she was frickin' gorgeous.

I had to glue my hands to my sides and stare into those beautiful brown eyes just to stop myself thinking about the way Evan had described her breasts.

"The British girl? She's got nothing on the girls around here, except for those milky-white, supple peaches."

Man, he thinks he's some kind of poet. I don't even want to think about what he writes in those love letters he's been sneaking to Anna-Mae.

"You need to get laid. Her name is Milly, and stop talking about her like that. It's not right."

He grins at me. "You *like* her."

"And" — I reach out and clip him behind the ear. Sometimes younger brothers need to be reminded of their place — "what's it any business of yours?"

"Daddy will pitch a fit if you even look in her direction. He has plans for you, and they don't include a British girl. I googled her. You should see how she dresses on stage. I would steer clear if I were you."

I can look at her. I can even talk to her if I goddamn want to.

Well, if my stupid brain decides to function this time, and I can get out more than three words, like a normal human being.

Evan's right. It's not like anything could ever come of it. I can hear my dad's voice saying, *"She's no good for you, son. You're a Booth, remember?"*

Mark Booth, self-elected head of this town — upholding the values of this place, like his daddy before him and his granddaddy before him. Be bold, be brave, lead by example.

If the example is cheating on Mama — sending her to the bottom of a bottle every night — and chasing anybody out of town if they don't fit the mold then, yeah, he's doing just great.

Makes me want to head on the next bus right back to the city. I should have stayed on after college, got a job, an apartment. I let myself get lured back here with promises of horses and a job then *boom*, before I know it, they've got their claws in and I'm stuck.

We draw up at The Clearing. Not many trucks in the parking lot. I must have driven here pretty fast. *Play it cool, Elijah. Breathe. She's just a girl.* A beautiful girl who looks and sounds like an angel.

Man, it would really help if I could stop thinking about the way Evan described her breasts.

Chapter Three

Milly

The girls and I all pile into a seven-seater van. I've got my own personal sauna going on under this dress and now I'm crammed up against six other people. This is the kind of thing that would test a solid friendship, let alone being with a group of people I've just met.

Without any parents around, I get to see what they're really like — chatty, animated, liberated…well, to a certain degree. Is it weird that I find myself wanting them to like me? Maybe it's because I'm far from home — or maybe they just seem nice.

"So, what's the gossip?" I take advantage of a lull in the conversation. My actual question should be *'Is Eli single?'* but this one will do for the moment.

"The gossip?" Mackenzie leans forward from behind me. "You mean boys?"

I chuckle. "Yes. Are you all dating?"

One of the girls whose name I can't remember breathes in through her teeth, shakes her head and smiles — like my math teacher used to do when I tried to answer any algebra-related questions. "Who's going to tell her?"

"Tell me what?" *Oh God.* That sounds ominous — and a little cultish.

"Yeah, we don't date." She giggles nervously, waiting for backup from her friends, but none comes. "I mean, we do, but it's way more complicated than kissing. We do dating with a purpose here, kind of like courting."

I swallow and do my best to hide my absolute shock at being in a car with a bunch of late teens, early twenties virgins. This is much worse than a cult. It's positively *chaste.*

"But you've kissed boys, right?" I could add *'or girls'* but I've already made the awkwardness in the car go up ten or so notches. Now is *"not the time to educate"*, as Sal would say.

They all turn and look at Raylyn, who is furiously blushing. She has definitely kissed a boy. "Yeah, some of us. We don't really talk about it."

"I'm sorry. I didn't mean to offend. Are any of you courting, then? Or about to be?" A couple of girls raise their hands.

"Addison and Anna-Mae are both in the early stages of courting," explains Mackenzie. I turn to listen, smiling at them to show my interest. The awkward in the air clears a little. I'm not going to judge — out loud, at least — and they get that. "That means that they are interested in a guy and he's interested in them, but that's as far as it has gotten. Maybe something will happen today."

"So it always ends in marriage?" I ask. What if the guy turns out to be a terrible person? You're stuck. You see, this is why I don't do any of this relationship stuff.

You never know who you're going to end up with in twenty years' time.

"No. Not always. At least you haven't wasted your kisses on him."

The conversation lulls again and I go back to looking out of the window. I'm surrounded by virgins, and it's very surreal. How am I supposed to fit in now? I've *'wasted'* a hell of a lot of kisses in my life...and more.

A smile creeps onto my lips. My mum would be so proud of me if she could see me right now. This is exactly the kind of thing she has always wanted—a certain degree of purity on my part.

Is that why Eli's so friendly? He's not getting anything from anyone else. Maybe he thinks he's going to get something from me? No, that's not fair. He's been nothing but gentlemanly. Plus, I wouldn't want him, anyway. I mean, yes, the way his jeans just hugged him in all the right places made my heart flutter, and yes, his self-assured, confident cowboy swagger is as sexy as hell, but I'm not looking to find myself a husband right now—or ever, for that matter.

And he's certainly not on the lookout for a non-virginal, pink-haired wife.

The cars head down a dusty lane and we park. Everybody piles out. They must have called friends because we're now a good thirty or so as we head toward The Clearing.

The boys, a rowdy group, are overexcited, pushing each other and making a lot of noise. Guess they need to get that frustration out some way or another.

I can't stop thinking about it. It's a different culture and I should be understanding of the way people choose to live their lives, but damn, it's so archaic.

These are the people I'm going to be serving coffee and cake to for the next few months, that's all. It's not like I can't date someone from the next town along or even from Austin. It's only forty-five minutes away. Then again, maybe a little forced celibacy will do me good. Perhaps my new normal could be a new, pure me.

I chuckle to myself. *Who am I kidding?* Some of the boys in the group are downright delicious. So many kisses that could have been wasted.

The Clearing lives up to its name. A short walk through the woods leads us to an open grassy area that leads down to the river. It's a shame that nobody is going to be stripping off and jumping in the water. It's not that kind of party.

I spot Eli. He's talking to one of the girls from the car. Taking advantage of my new-found friendship, I join them.

"Hey," says the girl. Behind the butter-wouldn't-melt smile on her face, she's gritting her teeth. *Am I interrupting something?*

"Hi."

Eli turns to look at me and greets me with a tilt of the head. I find it hard to shift my gaze from his eyes, again. He's so very handsome — and so fucking sure of himself. He looks at his feet, kicks at the dusty ground. He doesn't appear to be listening to what my friend says at all.

My stomach does that thing that means I'd quite like to be alone with this guy. I glance around us. The whole boy-girl separation thing still seems to exist, even out of their parents' sight. *Ugh. No fun.*

"So, what's the plan for the afternoon? We just hang out?" Everybody's just milling around. Without a drink in my hand or a man on my arm, I'm kind of lost.

Wow. The words *'basic bitch'* jump into my brain. Am I totally incapable of having innocent fun? College has spoiled me.

"Some of the guys are fixin' to play football. Evan always brings a pack of cards," replies the girl. Do they play poker? I doubt it, and that's the only card game I know how to play. She places a hand on Eli's arm, causing him to flinch. "Eli always plays football, don't you?"

He shrugs and shuffles her hand off his arm. Is it physical touch that repulses him or just this girl?

I reach into my bag. "I think I'll just read my book." She smiles at me and takes a cursory glance at the book in my hand. It's *The Testaments* by Margaret Atwood. She nods, as if she knows it well. I'm ninety-nine percent sure she has no idea what this book is about.

The conversation stalls, and realizing that she isn't going to get any more out of Eli, she wanders off, leaving the two of us alone. Settling down onto the hard, dry ground and opening my book, I expect him to wander off, too, but he moves next to me, close enough for me to feel the warmth of his thigh against mine.

I glance at our legs. "Should you be sitting so close?"

He grins cheekily. "I don't think anything could penetrate that dress."

"It is pretty thick." I don't know what Sal was thinking when she bought me this sack. The girls here are covered, but they still have light cotton summer dresses on. This one itches like it was weaved out of thick wool shipped over from a remote Scottish island that has never seen the sun.

"Do you mind?" His leg on mine? This might be the nearest thing to sex I'll experience for the next six months. I'm going to take anything I can get.

"Not at all, but I'm pretty sure the touchy-feely guards will be along any minute to put at least three feet between us."

He ignores my snarky remark and points at my book. "I preferred *The Handmaid's Tale*."

"You've read her books?" It's difficult to hide the surprise in my voice.

He grins. "Yes. Literature major." He leans a little closer. "I have Instagram, too. And TikTok. I'm a frickin' rebel." *All right, no need to tease.*

"I'm sorry. It's hard not to judge. You're all so different to what I'm used to."

He grins. "How?"

"You don't drink. You don't kiss. It's like kindergarten."

"It's a choice. We're not obligated. My mama brought me up to be responsible when it comes to people's feelings. I don't have to. Kyle, my brother... He's two years older than me. He went to college, joined a frat and never looked back."

"Is he single? Can I have his number?" I wink at him and the grin drops.

I've offended him. *Great.* "Nobody made you come here today."

"I'm sorry. My sense of humor is a little twisty at times. I'm intrigued by your lifestyle, though. Well, not yours personally, but everybody here. You've really never kissed a girl?"

He smiles, but he's taken aback by my bluntness, mouthing a *'wow'* at me. "A gentleman never tells." So he has? *Interesting.* Maybe he is a rebel, after all.

"Isn't it a little archaic? Somewhat misogynistic? You can't tell me that this kind of thing isn't about controlling women in so many ways. I couldn't think of anything worse. Stuck with the first person I kiss for the rest of my life? No, thank you."

He rubs his chin, scratching at the little tufts of blond stubble. "Like I said, nobody is *forced* to do anything." I raise my eyebrows. Does he really believe what he's saying? "Sure, it's expected of us, but it's not just the women. We men hold ourselves to high standards, too. We dress in a way that doesn't attract a woman's eye."

An unintentional cough erupts from my throat, and he squints at me. Can he tell I'm thinking about his bum in those jeans? Probably. "Sorry... Carry on."

"A vow of chastity is difficult for men, too. Not kissing someone you're attracted to is hard. Not touching someone is hard."

"Hard," I say, suppressing my giggles at his repeated use of the word.

"*Very* hard," he replies with a wink, and I let out a snort. I need to get away from this guy before the secret-sexual-attractiveness-police arrive. "Are you intrigued by my lifestyle or are you intrigued by me?" The grin is back.

"A lady never tells." I look at my book, avoiding his gaze. This conversation is over. I don't want to read. I want to observe, learn, but I want to do it slightly farther away from this man and the pheromones he is throwing my way.

He gets up and heads toward the footballers. Turning back to look at me, he says, "Gilead is fictional."

Sure. This place feels eerily close though.

My afternoon is spent reading, chatting and making friends. Despite all of them either working or studying, the girls and I arrange to meet up in the week for lunch and maybe a movie at some point. The politeness is taxing at times. I'm used to racier more irreverent conversation, but they're fun and sweet and I'm less alone in their presence.

Does this make me a bad person? Maybe I'm a reformed bad girl. Soon the only swears you'll hear me say are, *'gosh darn it'* and *'goodness me'*. My mother would absolutely die with joy.

* * * *

"Did you have a nice time?" asks Sal as she serves me my supper.

I sprinkle a little Parmesan over my bolognaise. "You sound like my mother."

She raises her eyebrows. Now she looks just like my dad. "And you sound like a surly teenager when you reply to me like that."

"Sorry. Yes, I did." I take a sip of water, roll my eyes and huff for effect. "How's Carrie?" My question is moot. We both know how bad it is.

"Tired. She has got another round of treatment in a week or so and that'll wipe her out even more." Sal is losing the love of her life, and I don't know how to make it better—because I can't. "So, did you meet any nice young men?" She stops short, squints at me. "You like men, right?"

I guess my reputation for telling men to fuck off when they propose precedes me.

I giggle. "Yes. Yes to your first and second question, not that it means anything. I'm far too..." Too what? Too much of a slut? Too horny? "Experienced. Plus, I'm not into dating for marriage. I'm not into marriage, full stop."

"I know," she replies winking at me. "And it's 'period'," she adds, wrapping her spaghetti around her fork

"What?"

"They say 'period' here, not 'full stop'. I didn't ask if you'd found a husband. You never know... You might surprise yourself and fall in love." And cement my feet to the floor in this dreary old town? *No thank you.* "What's his name?"

I feel myself blush. A smile forms on my lips and I can't wipe it. "Elijah."

"Booth?" Her fork clatters onto her plate. I lower my head, chastised. "Please be careful with the Booth boys, Milly. They have...power." Power to hide the body? Power to sweep crimes under the carpet?

"You make them sound so threatening."

She thins her lips, which is the grown-up symbol for *'this conversation is over'*, and we finish our food.

Somehow the thought that Elijah Booth might be a little bit dangerous makes him all that much more attractive. This quiet little town could do with a few more adventures.

"Be careful what you wish for," my mother likes to say. Sometimes wishes come true.

Chapter Four

Milly

Two nights later my phone vibrates. I almost jump out of my skin. It's eleven p.m. and I'm way down the deepest rabbit hole on YouTube watching something about unbelievably real photos of supposed time travelers.

What is Mackenzie doing calling me at this time of night?

"We need your help. Can you come pick us up?"

"Sure, where? Are you okay?" I look at my fleece pajamas. *Meh*, that's not going to cut it in this town.

"Fine. Please, just hurry — 1435 Millers Drive."

I creep down the stairs. Sal and Carrie are asleep, both exhausted. Sal's been letting me borrow the truck for little trips to get me used to driving over here. It's much better than the Pontiac. There's air conditioning, for a start. Grabbing the keys, I head out, sticking a little Post-it on the door. I don't want them to worry.

My phone leads me out of town and along a dusty road. There are a lot of dusty roads around here. Have they never heard of tarmac?

All at once I spot the problem. Somebody is having a party, and they haven't asked me. *Well, fuck.* This is a side of town I didn't know about.

The driveway is packed, so I pull up in front of the house. The girls aren't anywhere to be seen, so there's no option but to go in. *Really glad I ditched the pajamas.* Heading past the couple making out—in a very impure, unchaste way—on the front lawn, I enter the house through the wide-open front door. It's wide open because it's hanging off its hinges. This place is a wreck.

The house is packed. It's the late stages of a party that must have been going on all day. If they're not already making out with someone or trying to sleep in any available space, the guests are dancing to their own personal beat. Some kind of music, which involves one continuous drumbeat, is blasting, loudly, and there's an awful lot of red plastic cups everywhere. The stench of beer and weed hangs in the air. None of these people are my customers. They're certainly not from around here.

I've seen enough American TV to know that this isn't the kind of party that Mackenzie, Raylyn and their friends are used to.

I push through the people until I spot Elijah…Evan? No, neither. It's another Booth made from the same mold. He's helping several other friends hold some guy upside down with a funnel in his mouth.

"Kyle?" I call out.

He looks over at me, smiles, almost dropping his charge. "Yeah."

"I'm looking for Mackenzie, uh, I don't know her surname."

He laughs. "Upstairs bathroom." I smile my thanks and go to leave, but a fight has broken out and I am forced to stand and wait for them to finish.

A hand grips my arm, I stare at it, peel it off, finger by finger, turning to look up at whoever would dare to grab me. *Kyle*. "You're not from around here." He glances up to my hair. "What's your name, Pink?"

Sal's words echo in my head. "*Power*." I smile sweetly. How can I make myself as unattractive to him as possible? "I'm Milly—a close friend of Eli and Evan's." His grip releases and he turns away. I am no longer of any interest.

I find the stairs and go looking for the girls. They're huddled together, sitting on the bathtub, crying and acting like they've been taken hostage. The girl from the other day—Addison, or is it Anna?—is hunched over the toilet. She's a rather nasty shade of green and she has the distinct odor of someone who mixed their drinks and deeply regretted it.

"Have you been drinking?" I ask, sounding like my mum.

"Only Addy," replies Mackenzie. "I'm sorry."

"Hey, you do you. You're allowed to have fun." They shake their heads. This isn't fun for them. "Let's get you home. I'll take Addison back to my place. She can stay with me until tomorrow morning."

I pick up the invalid, hoist her arm over my shoulder and usher the girls out of the bathroom and down the stairs. They are out of that house in seconds, but Addison's walking skills have been seriously hindered and it takes me a while to get down. Plus, she's heavy and she smells like puke. This is not what I signed up for when I moved here. I'm normally the one being helped.

If I didn't have to drive, I might have stuck around and had a beer myself. I'm starting to forget what alcohol tastes like. *Criminal.*

At the bottom of the stairs, I plonk Addison on a chair and take a breather. Kyle walks by with a couple of friends. He's as gorgeous as his brothers, but there's something different about him — the same confidence as Eli, but with a touch of menace. Untrustworthy. I'm glad to be getting the girls out of there.

His friend bends over and sticks a finger under Addison's chin. "Whoa, we've got a live one here."

"Get your hands off her," I snap, pushing his hand away.

Kyle grabs my wrist, again. "This is my house. We do what we want here." He doesn't add *'know your place',* but I can sense that he has a habit of getting his own way with the women in his life.

I lean in and remove his hand a second time. "Fuck you…and your friends."

Kyle's shoulders rise and he breathes in, ready to retort. An arm pushes in between us and pulls me back away from Kyle. "Go to your truck, Milly," says Eli. I turn to look at him. He is glaring at me, his face like thunder.

"Addison," I reply, looking at her. He shakes his head and whisks her up into his arms, carrying her out through the front door.

"Where's your truck?" I point to where the other girls are waiting. They look traumatized, their eyes widening in joy as they see Eli carrying their friend to safety from this den of iniquity.

It's just a party, for fuck's sake. This is what you get when people are overprotected.

They open the door. He piles Addison in next to them, then turns to look at me. "Have you been drinking?" he spits, angrily.

"No." *Wait, what?* "I'm not... I wasn't..."

"You can't do things like this — just swan in and start taking them to parties and drinking. They never went to college. They're not like" — he hesitates. *Us?* — "you."

Right. Sure. I don't reply, bite my tongue. Of course he'd think that I'm responsible. I'm the pink-haired slut from England.

My lips part, ready to yell out a disparaging reply, but what's the point? He has already formed an opinion of me, just as I did with him the other day. My heart breaks a little. I was expecting to be judged by these people...but not by him. He'd been the normal one. There'd been flirting...hope, a hint of attraction.

I storm around the truck and jump in. "Let's get you girls home. That's more than enough excitement for one night." Revving up a little, I make very sure that my exit leaves him in a cloud of dust.

My hands are shaking. *Fear of Kyle or rage?* A bit of both. Sal was right. The Booth family is to be avoided at all costs.

I arrive home to flashing lights. *Shit.* Did Sal call the police? No, it looks like Carrie has taken a turn for the worse. I leave a sleeping Addison in the car and rush over to the ambulance.

"Is she okay?" Sal shakes her head. She looks older, thinner. I swear her hair has turned grayer overnight. "Go with her, and don't worry. I'll take care of the shop tomorrow. Stay with her. Keep me updated." She nods and the doors close, whisking my sweet Carrie off to hospital.

I look up at the stars as I stand in the silent driveway, soaking in the cool night air, allowing my heartbeat to slow. It's been a bit of a night. *If anybody up there gives a damn, please let Carrie make it through okay*. The urge to call my family hits me all of a sudden. A familiar voice, some inane gossip about one of the neighbors would be a welcome change from all of this. But they would only worry about Carrie or about me. I'm a grown-up now. I've got this.

Addison is sober enough now to walk into the house. I hand her a pair of pajamas, put her in my bed, stick her clothes in the washing machine and lay my tired body on the couch. It's not like sleep's going to come, anyway. Sal is losing her soulmate and she's doing it alone. I need to step up.

* * * *

Eli

I stand there in a cloud of dust, watching the truck drive away. What did I ever see in that girl? It's not something I say a lot, but my dad's right. I got sucked in by sweet perfume and a cute smile and didn't think about whether this girl was the right one for me.

Raylyn called me half an hour ago, begging me to come save her and the girls because they were "*trapped*" in the bathroom at Kyle's house. I look back at the house, taking in the devastation he has wreaked in this place. Dad is going to be pissed when he sees this. I'll have to come back tomorrow and help him get that door back on or he's going to get a hiding he won't see coming.

He won't learn. He never does. Kyle is the golden boy — the only one of us who can never do no wrong, until now. This might be a little too far. I'm not sure Momma and Poppa had this in mind when they gave him the house.

My brothers and I were right there. We could have taken this on as a project, built it into something amazing, but no, they had to give it to Kyle.

I kick at the dust, deciding whether or not to go back inside. Damn it. I'm so mad at Milly for letting me down.

It doesn't surprise me that she came to the party. I just don't get why she brought the other girls. They're not used to this kind of thing, especially drinking. And this place reeks of liquor and sex.

Milly might think I'm a boring, but I don't see the joy in drinking. I've seen firsthand how it ruins your life and I don't want that for me — or my future wife and kids.

I'm mad at myself for liking her and even madder for thinking she wasn't going to let me down, because that's what happens. You get close, you let someone in and they let you down.

Women are so damn confusing. I love my mom, but she has never been someone I've gone to for advice. I'm not even sure I'd want to take it. She sure does like dishing it out when she gets the chance, but I smile and do what I want to do, anyway.

I've tried to get close to girls in the past but… I don't know. Maybe I wasn't ready, or they weren't the one. I'm not saving myself for marriage, not anymore. I'm saving myself for someone I can trust. And Milly has just proved that I'm right to do it.

I head back to my truck and drive home — the air blasting to keep me awake. I can hardly keep my eyes open. I'll sort Kyle's mess out in the morning. Looks like he's going to need it.

My phone rings as I'm putting my key in the front door, and I leap back down into the yard so I don't wake up the whole household. "Hey," says Raylyn, "we're home now. Thanks for coming. I didn't know Mackenzie had called Milly, so sorry for getting you out of bed for nothing."

What? Oh my God. "Huh? She called Milly?"

She pauses. "Can you hear me okay? Are you still at the party?"

"No, I'm home. Did you say Milly wasn't at the party?" My heart sinks. *Damn it.*

"No. I feel real bad. Mackenzie's mom said they saw an ambulance going to her house about a half hour ago. She rang Sal, who told her that Carrie's been taken ill. She has to go into the hospital. Can you imagine? Milly didn't need us bothering her on top of that."

Fuck. She didn't need me shouting her, either.

"Thanks, Raylyn. Drink some water and get some sleep."

I hang up.

Any hope I ever had of having anything with Milly evaporated tonight. My stupid mouth got ahead of my brain. Seeing her getting pushed around by Kyle and his friends made me so mad. Nobody should be treating a lady like that. I saw red and said some things I shouldn't have.

We get told to respect women, and at the same time people like Kyle and my daddy — the most popular, outgoing people in my family — treat every lady they meet like a piece of shit. I shouldn't think like that about my own father, but it's true. He's telling me and my brothers to keep our distances and he has disrespected my mom for years.

I need to make it up to Milly. It's going to take more than an apology to get me out of this one. I'm going to have to dredge up some of that Booth charm we're all supposed to have. I'm pretty sure it skipped a generation when it came to me and my brothers, but heck, I'm willing to give it a try.

Chapter Five

Milly

The next morning I take Addison home. We had a sleepover at my house, I inform her. All the girls are in on the lie. With her clothes cleaned and dried, you couldn't even tell. Only her badly hidden hangover remains of their little adventure into life outside of their bubble.

I open the coffee shop, praying that I have the balls to pull this off. Shortly afterward, Harry trundles in and sits at his usual place. He's early today. His hand grips my wrist as I place his pie and iced tea on the table. He sighs, fixes my regard — tears forming in his eyes — and throws me a weak smile, but he is convincing nobody.

"Don't you cry, Harry. I'm barely holding it together as it is." The rumor mill in this town is overly efficient.

He manages a weak smile and the grip on my wrist loosens, but he is still holding on to me. This place is home for him, and Carrie is family. "She is so loved. She needs to know that."

"She knows." Sally and Carrie have the strongest, sweetest love of anybody I've ever met. Then there are all the townspeople who come to this place every day, just to sit and chat. If love can save you, then Carrie truly has everything going for her.

The irritating jingle of the door brings an unexpected visitor.

"Hi." Eli flashes me a conciliatory smile, as if it makes up for the previous night. "Thought you might need a hand today."

"I'm fine." I'm not, but he doesn't need to know that. "Thank you."

"You're not fine." *What the fuck?* "Look... I'm here for Carrie...if you want." Without even waiting for an answer, he jumps behind the counter, washes his hands and ties an apron around his waist. He inspects the coffee machine, tutting to himself, and gets to work setting it up. "Have you even turned this thing on yet?"

There's a tug on my wrist, and Harry winks at me, nods. "I guess if you're doing it for Carrie," I say, using the most cutting tone of voice I can muster in my tired state. This doesn't mean he's forgiven, but he's right. I do need the help.

The morning rush comes in around eight a.m., the queue going out of the door. Eli is a whizz with the coffee machine, loading and tapping and making all the right *ssh*-ing noises — all the while explaining to me how to do it.

"Lay everything out in a line, so it goes cup, cream or milk, sprinkles or cocoa, lid." I turn up the radio and we get a rhythm going. We even add the occasional salsa as we shimmy around each other. Despite myself, I'm starting to forgive him. We do make a good team.

The rush calms, the last customer is served and the place looks like a bomb hit it. I can hear Sal's voice in my mind, *'stock up, sweep up'*. I turn the radio to max and we get to work.

Dancing out of the storeroom, take-out cups in my hands, I shake them like maracas. He grabs them, puts them on the counter, then, forgetting himself for a moment, takes my hands and tangos me back into the storeroom until we're backed up against the wall.

"You've got moves," I say, laughing as he leans me back on myself. He blinks, his lips parted, catching his breath. Suddenly all too conscious that we're entwined in a backroom, our faces only inches apart, he jumps back, almost dropping me to the floor. "Hey, careful!"

Nobody has ever run out of a storeroom quicker than a Booth who almost kissed the pink-haired English girl. I straighten my clothes and follow him back out.

He hands me the perfect latte. "By way of an apology." He's leaning on the counter, giving me his best puppy-dog eyes.

"For what? The tango?" *Or nearly kissing me?*

"No...the assumption. I didn't know the girls went to that party on their own last night. Raylyn called me and told me what you did. I'm a dumbass."

I bob my head in agreement, leaning next to him, our elbows touching. "True." He looks away, makes a terrible attempt at hiding the smile on his face. "Your brother is something else — and not in a good way."

Flirting is so easy with Eli — gentle teasing, the brush of hand, the mating dance of the horny human.

"Would you believe he's studying law? Wild, right?" Somehow I can see his asshole of a brother defending other assholes in a court of law. He moistens his lips. He's doesn't want to talk about his brother right now. He's clearly got other things on his mind.

"And you... What are you going to do when you grow up?"

"Horse whisperer, singer-songwriter."

I laugh, but he's dead serious. "Oh, really? Sorry. I thought..."

He grins, totally confident in what he has just said. The man is a mystery to me, never doubts himself for a second. I've never met anybody so bold before, and it disturbs me. "I'd love to see that...all of that. Not at the same time, though." I lean back on the counter and he takes a step forward. Once again, I'm left wondering if he is going to kiss me.

He breathes in loudly and bites his lip—those baby blues staring straight into mine, melting me from within. "I'll sing for you anytime...or take you riding. I know you sing, but do you ride?"

"I've ridden." It comes out way sexier than I intend. His breath hitches. "I'm pretty good, actually," I add with a grin. He is so close that I can smell the coffee on his breath.

The door jingles. "Dad?" Eli is thrown. He searches around for something to look like he was doing—anything other than seduce me.

An older, wrinklier version of the Booth clones walks in. He tips his hat at me. "Ma'am." His eyes catch mine, but they are devoid of emotion. The friendly smile on his mouth is a lie.

I busy myself wiping down the counter as Elijah moves away from me. "Mr. Booth, how can I help you? On the house, of course."

He ignores me and looks over at his son. Polite conversation is over. Just like his eldest son, Booth Senior tolerates women only to a point. "Elijah, I'm going to need you back at work." It isn't a request. It is an order. Eli pales. *When Booth Senior speaks, you obey. Power.*

Eli grabs his stuff. "Are you going to be okay?"

"Fine. Thanks Eli...jah."

They leave without a goodbye. Carrie mentioned that she and Sally were tolerated in this town, and their pink-haired niece is clearly tarred with the same brush. I really need to do something with my hair. Not because of the people here, just because it's starting to look like a bird has nested on my head and I am the face of this coffee shop now. Time to look like I mean business.

I text Addison, firstly to check how she's feeling and secondly to get the name of a good hairstylist. I don't need a makeover. I'm not trying to impress a boy. *Right? Right.* I continue to lie to myself until I shut up shop and head to the salon at the end of a very long day.

* * * *

Eli

"That was rude."

"What?" My dad stands by the passenger side of my truck, his fingers gripping the door handle. I've been promoted to chauffeur. "Open the door. I have things to do."

"Back there... That was rude." He ignores me, as he always does when he thinks what I'm saying is inconsequential or just plain wrong. I get in the truck, start it up and choose the radio station. In my space, I have some semblance of control.

"Take me home, then I'm gonna need you to head over to Kyle's house. He had a few friends over last night and it got out of hand." *Understatement of the century.*

"You can say that again."

"You knew about this?" And there it is. Somehow this had to get around to being my fault.

"No, I heard." Thank the lord he doesn't know I was there, even if it was fleeting. It'd still end up being my fault.

Kyle is sitting on his front lawn on a couch that appears to have mysteriously made its way out of the house. I say sitting. It's more of a lean, as he sticks his tongue as far as it can go into some girl's mouth.

I cough. The girl is way more interesting than me. I bend down to his ear and shout, "Kyle!" He jumps three foot high. *Oops, I guess I scared him.* "Dad said you needed some help."

He peels himself off her. "Stop shouting, dickweed. I've got a headache. Grab a trash bag and get to picking stuff up."

Cool. This is *not* what I signed up for when I was hired to work for my dad's property management company.

Kyle's friend is adjusting her bra and I'm torn between being polite and looking at her wrong. "Ma'am." I tip my cap and stare at the ground. "How about I fix that door instead?" It's still hanging off its hinges, barely holding on. That beautiful wooden door welcomed me to Momma and Poppa's house more times than I can mention. My safe haven…now a drug haven. "You got tools? You and your friend want to take the couch back inside before I do it?"

He lifts his nose from between his partner's breasts and glares at me. "You might want to shut up, start picking up trash and be glad I haven't kicked your ass for shoving me last night when I was having a nice conversation with Pink."

Pink? My blood pressure rises a notch. My fists ball up. Punching him would feel great right about now, but it wouldn't do me, or Milly, any good to let Kyle know my feelings for her.

Especially as I'm not sure about my feelings for her myself.

I was so close to kissing her in the back room today. Man, I've managed to avoid putting my mouth on another person's mouth for twenty-one years, and it almost happened dancing with a girl I hardly know over a pile of paper cups.

Like it was the most natural thing in the world.

I've seen it when I was in college, almost felt it once or twice, but I've never actually one-hundred-percent wanted to do it.

I grab a bag and start throwing empty cups into it, distracting myself from the butterflies in my stomach and the feelings stirring inside me. People in this town have been thrown out of their homes for less exciting things than kissing pretty girls in storerooms.

I can't help it, though. I want to see her again. I want to tell her my dad's an ass, and I want to kiss her.

Fuck. I *really* want to kiss her.

I throw another few cups in the bag. I'm going to need a plan.

Chapter Six

Milly

Sal's town is kind of how I imagined small-town life in America. There's a main street with lots of small independent businesses and there are larger shops on the outskirts. It's very rural here, not something I'm used to. Even in the countryside in the UK you're not far from some of the bigger towns. This place feels like it's stuck in the middle of nowhere.

Back home people consume. We buy and we buy, and we eat and we eat. You can never find a decent enough excuse not to go to the pub on a Friday with your friends. Here, you have everything you need, but life is a little less frenzied. There are more crafts shops than there are bars. If I ever wanted to go into quilting, I would be spoiled for choice.

The hairdresser's salon is at the end of Main Street. Going by the voice on the phone, I had this image of a middle-aged woman with blonde bouffant hair, but it's run by two beautifully coiffed and made-up women who look barely older than me. Their long hair is on point.

The salon is as modern as the coffee shop, and I chastise myself, once again, for imagining that small-town America would be stuck in a time-warp.

Kaylee, my hairstylist, sits me in a comfortable chair, runs her fingers through my mop and tuts. She breathes in through her teeth and rolls her eyes at her companion. "Who did this to you?" I don't have to be the slightest bit empathetic to realize that she is condescending as hell.

I scrunch up my nose and shift my weight in the chair. "A hairstylist, on a shoot, but it was a while back."

She makes an '*mm-hmmm*' sound and smiles at me again via the mirror. "Well, we can't leave it like this. Have you thought about extensions?" Reaching over to grab a magazine, she opens it up and shows me a woman with long wavy blonde hair. "Like this."

It does look kind of nice. "Maybe a bit shorter... Can I keep the color, at least partly?" From the look on her face, I'm not making any friends here.

Nevertheless, she starts gathering equipment and flashes a withering look at her colleague. "So, what brings you to town?"

"I'm running Carrie's coffee shop while she is" —I hesitate. *How public is Carrie's illness?* —"unable to do it herself."

Her finely manicured hand lands on her chest and she starts to fake cry, like she's just won Miss Texas. "Oh my, those poor ladies. That is so very kind of you." I sort of hope, in a slightly selfish way, that her fondness for my unselfish act extends to a reduction in the cost of this hairstyle, because I'm almost out of cash. "Are you a...*friend* of theirs?"

I know what she means, but I'm not going to rise to it. The antiquated views in this town are starting to rile me up, but I know better than to argue with someone who is about to cut my hair. "No, Sal's niece."

Two older women come in, bringing a blast of warm evening air into the salon and moving the conversation away from me. They look like they can't wait to spill the beans on something scandalous, throwing off their coats and settling into two empty chairs. Kaylee does her magic on my mop of hair, while I lean back and listen in, finally getting to hear some actual gossip.

Kyle's party is the subject of the day. His grandparents gave him the home he did his best to destroy the previous night, and apparently the Booth family is not amused. The two women both work for the Booths. That's not surprising, seeing as the family must make up seventy-five percent of the town's population.

"That boy is going to be the death of his parents," laments one of them, settling her curler-filled head under a dryer.

"I told Theresa when she had Jake that with four boys so close together, she was going to have her hands full. She's so proud of her babies she can't see past their faults. Evan can't even speak to you without blushing and hiding under his hat, and Elijah? All that boy wants to do is sit under a tree with a guitar all day." My ears prick up when I hear Eli's name mentioned, and I lean in a little more to hear her better. I catch Kaylee's eye in the mirror and she winks at me.

God, Milly, you're so obvious.

The other woman lifts her hand in agreement. "I can't see their daddy fixing to let one of his boys head on up to Nashville. Law and politics, that's the role of a Booth boy."

Whoa. Horse-whispering country-singer is not in either of those fields. Poor Eli. Overbearing parents suck. I should know. Well, that's not entirely fair. Mum nags and moans, but she still lets me do what I want. Okay, so I got an HND in English literature that has so far led me nowhere in life, instead of getting *"a real job"*, as Mum puts it, but at least I was allowed to fuck up my life all on my own.

The conversation moves on to people I don't know, and I move on to getting my new color rinsed. Lying there as Kaylee massages my scalp, my eyes glaze over. I've only had a couple of hours sleep and the nervous tension of this whole week has been exhausting. Every muscle in my body starts to melt into the chair. This is the most relaxed I've been since I got here.

Within an hour I'm all finished and looking spectacular. Kaylee has done a fantastic job, my hair shines and springs up like a shampoo advert. It's almost lengthy enough for me to look like I belong to the long-haired-virgin club, but it's still a very unconventional pastel pink.

My inner rebel is irked by my approach toward conformity, but as I flounce down the street, checking out my reflection in the shop windows, I like what I see. At the very least, I'm prettier than I was a few hours ago. My confidence is off the charts.

Chapter Seven

Milly

Sadly, there's nobody around to see it. It's getting late in the afternoon, all the shops are closed and I'm going home to an empty house. Sal texted me to say that there was no change and that she is staying by Carrie's side tonight. Nobody is allowed to visit because of germs, so I'm to feed myself.

It's such a waste to feel this amazing and have nobody to share it with. I pick up my phone to call the girls, but I'm tired and they probably are too. A selfie on Instagram will have to do. Some recognition of my gloriously beautiful mane is needed before I sleep on it and go back to looking like plain old me again tomorrow. It hasn't escaped my notice that both Eli and Evan follow me on there now, and within seconds, several little hearts appear in my comments.

Soppy-Girly-Milly wins over Rebellious-Single-Milly, and I gush a little at the fact that a boy liked my post. My day is made. Now I can have some dinner and finally get a good night's sleep.

The sound of messages landing on my phone wakes me. I didn't even make it to my bed, didn't even eat before crashing out. The couch is starting to become my new home. It's so comfortable and warm under my blanket that I don't even know if I want to pick up my phone and see why somebody wants to once again make me do something in the chill of the night.

Hey, it's Eli. I'm outside. Can we talk?

I peel myself off the couch and peek through the curtain. He's standing in front of the house, twiddling his thumbs and kicking at the dust. *Nervous as hell.* So the unnerving confidence is only in front of me, huh?

I crack open the door. "Hey, you guys really have to stop bothering me in the middle of the night and let me get some sleep."

His brow furrowed, he looks at me like I've lost it. "It's eight-thirty."

It is? *Shit.* I've only been asleep for an hour. *Awkward.* I open wider and lean into the doorway, reaching my hand up to my head as I remember that I have great hair today. "What can I do for you?"

"It looks nice. Your hair...I like it. I'm glad you didn't..." *Morph into one of the virgin brides?* Too late, the transformation has begun. I've only been here a week, my hair has grown drastically longer and I have hardly had any physical contact with someone of the opposite sex. It won't be long before I'm quilting myself a chastity belt.

"Thank you. Eli, why are you here?"

He takes a step forward. "Can I come in?"

"I don't know, can you? Is that allowed? There's nobody here." I wiggle my eyebrows, suggestively.

"I'm a grown-ass man, Milly. I can do what the fuck I like, unless *you* don't want me to come in." I haven't heard a single person swear since I got here, but Eli has already cursed in front of me twice today and now he's bringing out the big guns. "Sorry. I didn't mean to – "

"Go ahead. Don't mind me." I smile up at him, move out of the way to let him in. He takes his hat off and puts it on a side-table. This is the first time I've seen him without either a cowboy hat or a cap on his head. His hair is longer than I thought. An unruly curl tumbles in front of one eye and he pushes it aside. My stomach does a backflip, and I lean back against the wall to steady myself. That might be the sexiest thing I've ever seen.

Telling me I can't have sex has turned me into a horny little bitch.

I tighten my fists and dig my nails into my palms, resisting the urge to run them through his hair.

He hesitates, ruffles his hair again and I die a little inside. "I wanted to apologize."

"Twice in one day? It must be exhausting doing me wrong all the time." I flash a cheeky grin. Teasing him is so much fun.

"My dad was rude to you this morning, and I'm sorry about that. People from here don't like strangers." *And men from here don't respect women…present company excepted.* "But he shouldn't have ignored you like that. I've spoken to the girls and they're going to come help you. They won't be able to do the coffee like I can. I worked in Starbucks when I was in college. At least you won't be on your own." He's rambling and nervous, and it's cute as heck.

"That's so kind. Thank you. Would you like something to eat or drink? I... Uh, I haven't had time to eat yet. I fell asleep."

He slips off his boots and strides on through to the kitchen. "Well then, it looks like we're going to have to rustle you something up. You can't run a business on an empty stomach." He opens the refrigerator and rummages around. "Chicken salad?"

"Sounds good to me." I grab a chopping board and we get to work, side by side. His hands are big—masculine, if you will—but the deftness with which he holds and slices the tomatoes is as delicate as a three-star chef.

What else could he do with those fingers, given the chance?

He catches me staring, and a wry smile forms on his lips. "We'll be eating at midnight if you can't concentrate on the job at hand."

I scrunch up my nose, a failed attempt at hiding the warm blush that rises in my cheeks. "Sorry, I was..."

"Captivated by my skills in the kitchen? I get that a lot." I chuckle and tap my shoulder against his. "Hey, careful. Don't want to lose a finger," he adds.

How is this so comfortable? So easy? If I didn't know better, I'd think I was falling for this forbidden man's charms. *Pull yourself together, Milly.*

A few minutes later we plate up a decent meal. There's an open bottle of chardonnay in the fridge door. I've never noticed it before. Sal hasn't had a drink in front of me since I got here, but I don't blame her for cracking open a bottle at a time like this. I hold it up. "Do you want a glass? Oh no, you don't drink."

He shakes his head. "No, thank you."

I stand there, bottle in hand, wondering whether it would be impolite to serve myself some. I could certainly do with a drink.

"But you go ahead."

"You don't mind?"

He furrows his brow. "Why do you care what I think?"

He's right. Why do I care? I serve myself a glass and we sit at the counter. The sexual tension from this morning has fizzled down to camaraderie, as if neither of us quite knows how to continue where we left off.

I take a sip and let the chilled dry wine sink into my veins. "Why don't you drink? I mean, why does nobody drink around here?"

"I don't know. At college there were two types of people—those who drank a lot and those who didn't touch a drop. There was never an in-between. Being drunk around here is seen as really bad. You can lose your job or your friends, so people just don't do it at all. It's healthier that way, anyway, as alcohol isn't good for anybody. Do you think I should drink?" He spikes a piece of lettuce and eats it while he awaits my reply, his gaze never leaving mine.

I rest my fork on the side of my plate and grab my glass. "No. God. You do you. I'm just intrigued. Where I come from it's really rare to meet someone who doesn't drink at all, and that's more often than not because they've had a drinking problem. I suppose I thought it was normal to drink, but now I'm looking at it from your point of view. I can see why you don't."

"In the short while I've known you, you've interrogated me on my love life and my drinking habits. Anything else intensely private you want to know?"

How would his lips taste when they brushed against mine? "Your music. Sing me a song."

"Can I finish my salad first?" he replies, winking at me. "And I guess I could ask you to do the same. Sing, I mean."

"Oh, you can find me on the Internet with a simple search." *Oh shit.* Why did I say that? *Please don't.* I'm not UK Milly anymore. I'm US Milly. The new me doesn't have to live the eternal shame of being the woman who leaped over the sobbing man.

He squints at me, as if he's trying to penetrate my thoughts. "I want to hear your real voice."

I shake my head. "How about you ask me something private instead." *Ah, that got his attention. Conversation successfully steered.*

"Ooh, what do I want to know about you?" He scours my face. "What do you think about love, Milly, if you don't believe in marriage or soulmates?"

Oh. So he *has* seen the video. Guess that was too good to be true.

I smile, working out what I'm going to say next. "That's a pretty huge assumption on your part — that I don't believe in forever love. You're right, I suppose, when it comes to me. I don't do love. It's not my thing. It's too complicated, too much like hard work."

He puts down his fork and looks me dead in the eyes. "Wow. Eat up your salad then. You're going to need your energy."

"I am? Why?"

"All that hard work you're going to do when you fall in love with me." He's deadly serious. The confidence of this man. *Bless him. I'm going to break his sweet, sweet heart.*

We finish our meals in polite conversation, head out back to sit on the porch swing and enjoy the calm summer night. Sal and Carrie's house is so far from town that you can just about see every constellation in the sky. The chirping crickets and the occasional scuffling and neighing of the neighbor's horses getting a last run in before settling in for the night punctuate the evening air. There's a certain magic in this place. Warm nights and good company... What more could you want from life?

"You're so sure I'm going to fall in love with you. What about me? What makes you think you'll fall in love with me?"

"You have a kind heart. You flew across the world for your aunties. You wore that potato sack to the party out of respect, and you didn't think twice about helping Addison the other night. You're feisty, too. Plus, you're beautiful. That's for sure a point in your favor."

"And you're a charmer. Nobody's ever called me 'feisty' before. Stubborn and pigheaded, maybe."

"Nobody's ever told my brother to *fuck off* before...certainly no woman." He swears just like me, in a terrible English accent, making me smile.

"True. You promised me a song."

He shakes his head. "I don't know. I don't even have my guitar."

"Excuses, excuses. Sing for me. Make me fall in love with you, Eli Booth." He taps his foot and breaks into a song about the most beautiful girl in the world. I've heard it before, but never like this. His voice is deep, soulful. For someone who has never been in love, he sure can break your heart with his words.

I sway to the music, leaning into him, my head finding comfort on his shoulder as he wraps his arm around me. The stress of the last couple of days catches up with me. Tears roll down my cheeks and settle on my lips.

He stops singing and bends his head toward me, the deepest blues eyes gazing into mine. Whenever we are together, I'm the only thing he sees. And I sink a little deeper every time.

He lifts my chin with his finger as he wipes my cheek with his thumb. Our faces are so close, the tips of our noses brushing against each other.

"May I kiss you, Milly?"

I refuse, back away.

He tips his head to one side, his face a picture of confusion. "Don't you want me?"

Oh, if he only knew how much I want him right now, how every nerve in my body is aroused by his very touch.

"I want to. I *really* want to, but..." Guilt rules over desire. "I can't let you waste your kisses on me. I can't stay here. I know that's not what you want. You'll want more than I can give you."

He scowls, hurt. "How the fuck do you know what I want?"

"I'm sorry. I didn't mean..."

"No, I'm sorry. I want you, Milly." He lowers his voice to almost a whisper, as if the whole town can hear us. "I've never wanted to kiss any woman in my life as much as I want to kiss you. I want my first one to be with you."

Oh my God, the pressure. "Your first kiss? Eli, I couldn't. I mean, yes, of course, but what if it's terrible and that's the only memory you have of me? A disaster of a first kiss that you're going to remember for — "

He presses his mouth onto mine and I glide back. He tastes like ranch dressing and wanton desire. The kiss is everything I've imagined every time I've looked at his face — gentle and yet firm. I pull away, take a breath and dive back onto his soft, warm lips, devouring him. He reaches around, gently holding me to him. He is savoring every second.

It's not terrible or dreadful. It's beautiful...full of grace.

He climbs over my body, the two of us lying on the swing as it rocks back and forth, his mouth not letting go for a second. He hardens against me. I want more. I want to rip his shirt from his jeans, run my hands over his tight warm body, but I resist.

We've already gone too far.

I can't take from him that which he is supposed to share with the woman he spends his life with.

I've already taken enough.

He pulls away, his breath rapid, his face flushed. His heart is beating so hard against my chest that it almost hurts.

"You broke your vow for me," I gasp, staring into those strong-willed eyes.

"Yes," he whispers, breathless, scouring every inch of my face, seemingly storing the memory of this moment forever in his mind. "Yes."

* * * *

Eli

Holy shit. No wonder it's not allowed. I didn't know one little kiss was going to have such an effect on me.

Can she tell? Can she feel it? I'm lying on top of her, so she has to know.

I want to kiss her again, but I don't know if my pants are strong enough to contain what's happening down there. I shift my weight. The only way to hide this boner is by sticking my hand down my pants, but I don't think that's going to make the situation any less uncomfortable than it already is.

She must think I'm such a virgin. I know I am, but my dick doesn't have to act like I'm sixteen again.

I've imagined this moment, my first real kiss, but it was always at the altar with my whole family watching. *Shit.* Can you imagine if this happened there? Nah, it can't be the same. You can't have this need, this longing in front of hundreds of people. This is the kind of thing you feel when you're alone with a woman.

That's exactly why being unescorted isn't allowed, either.

We're brought up to respect women, to keep our distance. We don't talk about it—masturbation, sex. They don't even warn us about getting hard until it happens when you least expect it and you have to hide it away. It's all a big secret, until your *special* day—your perfect virginal wedding.

I've been close to a woman but never like this— feeling her body against mine, doing things to me that I can't control, the smell of her perfume, the touch of her skin, wanting her so bad that it hurts and knowing that everybody thinks that it's wrong.

Forbidden…for some godforsaken reason.

How can something that feels this good be so bad?

"Eli, are you okay?"

No, ma'am. "Mm-hmm." *Fuck.* I'm literally lying on top of a beautiful woman and all I can do is think about weddings and jerking off. And my bone-a-thon is still going. I'm such a loser.

"It was really good. You don't need to look so scared."

"I…" *I, what? I'm sorry about my cock pressing into your thigh?* I stare down between us, trying to will it into submission. "I'm not…scared. It's…"

"Oh. *Oooh*, don't worry about…*that*. Eli, you know I'm not a virgin, right? It's not a problem. Really, it's kind of flattering."

Damn, woman, you are not *helping*.

I lift my hip and try to get it off her. "I'm sorry."

She brings her hand to my mouth, traces my lips. "Stop. It's totally normal. Enjoy it." Then she rests her hand on my cheek, brings her lips to mine and kisses me again. My body relaxes into hers and everything is as it should be.

I knew it when I saw her the very first time. I knew she was the perfect woman for me, and I knew I wanted to kiss her and *only* her.

And now I know why.

Chapter Eight

Milly

Opening the coffee shop has become second nature to me now. Only one week in and I am mastering the art of making a decent cup of coffee, picking up the pies and pastries from our supplier and running the place with a certain degree of efficiency.

It's not exactly teeming with customers, but those who do dare to come and try one of my lattes appear to be pleased enough with their purchase.

Raylyn — with two Ys — is waiting in front of the door when I arrive. She's my third assistant this week, not counting Eli. He didn't just help, he taught me how to run the place — and looked hot while he was doing it.

She flashes me the biggest smile and I throw one right back at her. It's a good feeling to have friends. "Are you my helper today?"

"Looks like it. Eli said you needed a hand." An even bigger smile creeps onto my lips as she mentions his name. Am I blushing? I'm probably blushing. That stolen kiss was special, but I can't allow myself to even hope that anything further will happen. And I'm pretty sure I'm not supposed to talk about it.

Ever.

With anyone.

Especially not the girls in this town.

We deal with the morning rush, and at about nine-thirty there's finally a lull. Raylyn has been amazing. She's not complained once, despite me being a terribly disorganized boss. The washing-up is piled in the sink, about to topple over any moment, and the coffee shop itself is a complete shambles.

I hand her a well-deserved iced tea. "Are we still on for a movie or something this week?"

She taps my arm in excitement. "Even better, Anna-Mae is preparing to announce her courtship. We're planning a party to celebrate."

"Who's the lucky guy?" I cross my fingers behind my back. *Please, don't let it be Eli.* Not only because of my growing feelings for him but because I think Anna-Mae is lovely. Female solidarity and all that. I don't want to go around stealing kisses from other women's boyfriends.

Oh my God. This place is turning me into a completely different person. I used to have the philosophy that if a guy wasn't dating then he was easy pickings—well, if he was into me, too. Now I'm seriously second-guessing as to whether anybody I even look in the direction of is spoken for, and even then, I keep my flirting to myself. I'm turning into a nun. *What is this sorcery?*

"Evan," she replies. I grin a little too widely and cover it up by jumping up and down and getting all excited.

Aren't they a little young, though? Eli's twenty-one and Evan has to be a couple of years younger than his brother, at the very least. It's easy to get confused here. When I arrived, I thought my friends were in their early twenties. They all dress like grown adults. There's little to differentiate between a sixteen-year-old and someone my age. And they all live such healthy lives — no cigarettes, no alcohol, not the faintest scent of weed. God, I must look ancient standing among them.

"How old are they?"

Raylyn squints and thinks about it for a second. "Evan is nineteen and Anna-Mae's eighteen. Yeah, she was eighteen in April. They've been fixin' to announce it for a while, but they wanted to wait until she was older." She goes on to explain the process — how they'll 'date' for a while, and if it works out, he'll ask her to marry him. They could be courting or engaged for another couple of years yet.

It's still so very young — for me, anyway. These guys are not fazed by it at all, and why should they be? The cement is mixing from the day they are born. They just have to find the right shoes and they're glued to the floor forever. A shudder runs down my spine at the mere idea of it.

My mum was the same — and most of my family. We're not so different, Raylyn and me, in what's expected of us. There's no courting ritual, no chaste vow, but once you're with someone, the pressure is on to settle down then have kids or get married or buy a house. Anything that makes splitting up that much harder.

"So, what about you?" I ask. "Any boys caught your eye?"

She shakes her head. Raylyn is shy by nature. Meek and mild. That's half the reason I was surprised to see her on the doorstep this morning. She'll need someone who is prepared to make the first move...and the second and the third.

"Oh no. Well, there was one guy, Scott. He... We were very close, but he's not from here."

The insinuation is clear. "Not suitable?"

"He kissed me." She blushes, as if she's just announced the most terrible sin.

"Did you kiss him back?"

She thwacks me on the arm. "Milly! As if. I'm not like that."

Like what? "Did you love him?"

"Yes." Her gaze sinks to the floor, and she runs the tea towel in her hands through her fingers. "Very much."

"You're an adult, you know. You can do what you want, despite what you're made to believe."

"I know, but I also love my friends and family very much, and they wouldn't approve." Familial approval is the crux of this issue for many of the young people around me. Their desires, their instincts are held back in the hope that they won't let everybody down.

At home we get mixed messages. My parents thought it was just the cutest thing that I had a boyfriend at nursery when I was four. Then at twelve, Kelly Woods kissed a boy and the race to kiss someone, anyone, before any of us was the last one to kiss a boy was on. At sixteen I was on stages singing about heartbreak and dressing and acting like I was already having sex. It wasn't long before that was the case. And yet the minute we get to our twenties the theme of the game changes. Find a man, settle down, have a couple of kids. Maybe get a dog, buy a house, get a part-time job.

These guys skipped the fun bit and went straight to the part where you feel guilty if you don't find a spouse, and you feel guilty if you do and you haven't done it properly. I was not well-placed to complain. Both of us had our issues, but hers clearly weighed on her more. The other girls knew about the kiss. They'd mentioned it that first time. I was grateful that Raylyn had her crew. She had people she could share with. How terrible if she had had to bear the burden of her guilt alone for a simple stolen kiss.

I stick a friendly hand on her shoulder. "You should do what makes you happy." My stolen moment with Eli is foremost in my mind. "That's my philosophy, anyway. I mean it constantly gets me in all kinds of shit, but, hey, that's life."

"What about you?" she asks, putting her glass into the dishwasher. "Met any guys that take your fancy?" I want to tell her. I want to gush over the perfect kiss with Eli, and how his mouth felt on mine.

That single unruly curl, and my desire to grasp onto it, seeps into my thoughts. My insides do a celebratory leap of joy at its very existence.

What a fucking mess. Raylyn had told me her secrets, and I still kept mine close to my chest.

I purse my lips. "No, nobody in particular." Sal doesn't need any more problems at the moment and me getting down and dirty with one of the Booth boys is probably about the worst trouble I could get myself into around here.

She smiles sympathetically, as if that's such a tragedy. "Maybe you'll meet someone nice at Anna-Mae's party."

"Maybe," I reply, "and maybe I'm not quite what the men around here are looking for in a girl." My reply stings more than it should. I'm most definitely *not* what Eli must have imagined his first girlfriend to be. And I never will be.

"No, what? You're amazing. You've had this incredible life already and you're so strong and brave. You flew across the world to a place you've never seen. You're so kind. I swear you terrified me that first day with your hair and your attitude." She brushes a lock of my hair from my eyes, like a mother to a child. "I wish I could be half the person you are."

"Aww. Raylyn, you are so sweet." She smiles at me and I hate myself even more for not telling her the truth.

I grab a cloth and head off to wipe the tables. This conversation is making me feel bad. I was supposed to be coming over here for adventures, not falling in love with the first boy I kissed and making friends who I don't want to leave behind.

Damn it. I'm so disappointed with myself right now.

Carrie is never far from my thoughts. When Sal texts me to say that Carrie's fever is down and she's coming home, I'm overjoyed. Then I remember that I haven't done shit in the house since they left.

I close the coffee shop at four, thank Raylyn for her help and rush home to get the house looking and smelling like somewhere someone might want to live.

* * * *

The washing-up at home is as bad as it was in the shop. I never signed up for dishes, and yet that's all I do. I haven't done a thing in the kitchen since Eli came over. His plate and his glass are still sitting on the counter waiting to be transferred into the dishwasher. Would he still be so enamored with me if he knew how lazy I've become?

My lips tingle at the memory of his mouth on mine, and I rub my finger along them, trying to stir the memory of how it felt. I have never been in love, and I'm not going to start now.

Just because I'm Eli's first kiss means nothing.

Just because he chose me when he could have had his pick of any of the single women in this town means nothing.

Every nerve in my body reminds me that the hill I chose to die on, the one with a big sign on the top that says *'we do not do love here'* is tricky to climb.

I'm going to be gone in a couple of months, maybe sooner. There will be no broken hearts when I leave, just fond memories and new friends.

I decide to change Carrie and Sal's bedsheets. Nothing like a clean room to come back to when you're feeling poorly. And I call my mum, because I like to torture myself occasionally.

Three points if she's still convincing herself that Carrie is Sal's best friend. Ten points if she mentions meeting a nice boy. A thousand bonus points if she asks me when I'm coming home.

"Milly, sweetheart, nice of you to call your mother." Ah, the guilt trip. Should have included *that* in the points system.

I pull off the sheets and roll them up into a ball. "Yes, but I've been running the coffee shop for Sal. Carrie had to go into the hospital for a few days."

"Oh dear. Sal is so nice, helping her friend out like that." And there it is. My eyes roll back into my head.

Seriously, Mum. It's not like Sal hasn't lived with her *'friend'* in the same house for twenty or so years.

Sal showed me where she keeps the clean sheets when I arrived. I grab everything I need and balance my phone on top. "Yes, she's a saint. So, how's everybody at home?"

"Well, your nan sends her love. She's been feeling a bit poorly herself lately, got a funny feeling in her legs." That'll be a side effect of the large quantities of gin that my dad's mother drinks behind Mum's back. "So, have you made any friends yet? Any special friends your mother should know about?" Two for two. Mum is on a roll.

"Yes, actually a couple of friends even helped me with the shop this week." *One of them helped me clean my mouth with his tongue.*

She pauses. "No nice boys, then?"

I sit on the bed hugging a pillow in my hands. "Oh, lots. Unfortunately, I'm not a nice girl, so that's that."

"Oh, sweetheart, you're going to make someone a lovely wife one day." Out of cardboard? Knitted? I could probably make one with dirty dishes if you give me a couple more days. "You know, Steve's back in town, if you're planning on coming home soon." We have a winner. Your prize is a date with Steve, the next-door neighbor's son who tried to touch your boobs under a table at a street party in 2013.

"Thanks, Mum, but I'm going to be sticking around for as long as Sal needs me." *And then some.*

I listen to twenty more minutes of family gossip then let my mum go. It's late at night in the UK and she's off to bed. I do miss her. I'm not a monster. But I'm also a grown woman with a life to live. She gets that, right? Underneath her unflappable desire to see me married and living down the street, popping out babies every couple of years.

I'm sure she loves me just the same.

Chapter Nine

Milly

Carrie has been back for two days. She is drained and tired, but Sal tells me that the doctors are optimistic. This spark of hope fills our little house with joy, and Sal and I dance around their bedroom to Whitney Houston, Carrie's favorite singer, while I tell them about the coffee shop and my new friends. It's little moments like this that make this house feel like a home. I'm starting to get ever-so-slightly attached.

My invitation, by text, to Anna-Mae and Evan's party has arrived, and Sal insisted that I get some more new clothes. She delighted in driving me to the mall, out of town, and we found so many summer dresses that are far prettier than the last one she bought me. They're still past the knee and covering my shoulders, but the necklines are a little more flattering. She tried to convince me to buy some pretty shoes to go with them, but I ended up with low-style Converses as a compromise. You can take the girl out of jeans, but you can't make her wear heels.

I'm loath to admit that I'm actually excited about going. The text chain is filled with updates on who's going to be there and what everybody is going to wear. I have inched my way into these people's trust, and this little community is growing on me.

"You sure you don't want to come?" I ask, sitting down at their dressing table and rifling around in Carrie's jewelry box for a pair of earrings.

"No, Carrie's not up to it, and I want to stay here to make sure she's okay." I know they just want some alone time. They've been in the kind of mood that makes teens cringe...all cuddly and lovey-dovey. I'm glad to be getting out of the house, to be honest.

I pick out a pair of little jade earrings and stand up to show the aunties my outfit. Carrie applauds, and I take a bow. I love these guys so much.

"Well, enjoy your night in. Don't wait up for me. I hear that Evan and Anna-Mae are having a butt-chugging competition, then it's orgy time on the south lawn."

Carrie rolls her eyes. "Be good. Stay away from the cute guys in the cowboy hats." She winks at me and pulls Sal down next to her, flicking on the TV and lining up their evening's viewing. That's my cue to leave.

"Love you," I say as I head downstairs.

"Love you, too," they reply, already forgetting that I was even there. I swear those two only have eyes for each other. They almost make me want to believe in love. *Almost.*

As I draw up in front of the Booth house, once again, my heart flutters. I fumble around straightening my skirt and fluffing up my hair. *Play it cool, Milly.*

Remember, he's not yours. I've never been in an illicit relationship before. I'd imagined it to be way more exciting, not as stressful. It's not like he's married or anything, and it was just a kiss. Well, it wasn't just a kiss. It was so much more.

Oh, for fuck's sake, I really need to get a grip.

I grab the pie I made from Carrie's recipe. Okay, so I filled Carrie's homemade pastry with apples and sugar. I still made it. It's not like I bought the damned thing.

If my friends could see me flouncing into the party with my bouncy hair and my dress and my pie, they would crack themselves up. But this is my new normal. I'm still rock and roll underneath.

As if to prove this point, I step in a pile of dog mess as I'm heading toward the buffet table and instantly forget to censor my reaction.

"Crap." Heads turn. Eyes widen. "Fuck. I mean, sorry. Um…" My gaze catches Booth Senior, who snarls in disgust at my fruity language. A hand grabs my arm. Thank God for Eli, coming to save me again.

I whirl around, expecting to see his familiar face, and find his mother staring back at me instead. She has the same curly blonde hair as all her sons — only it falls in ringlets down her back — and the deepest blue eyes. Surely she can't be a Booth, too, can she?

She flashes me the biggest, sweetest smile and mutters, through her teeth, "Stop cursing and let's get that shoe cleaned up." Turning to an awkward, lanky teenager standing beside her, she barks, "Jake, pick this mess up. And check that there aren't any more while you're at it."

I slip off my shoe at the doorway. "Thank you," I say as she leads me into the house. Her hand is gripping so hard on my arm that it's starting to cut off the circulation. Is this it? Is this the moment where I get dragged off to some secret lair, only to come out a couple of hours later with a fixed smile on my face and purity in my heart?

Turns out she's only taking me through to a laundry room. There are no torture devices, no chastity belts. Looks like we're good.

I sit on a machine while she rinses my shoe.

"So, you're Milly." What does she know? I give her a nervous smile, as I try to rub her finger marks off my arm. That woman has quite a grip. "Open up that cabinet behind your head, would you, darlin'?" She points behind me and I lean back and pull it open. "Now push the detergent out of the way and hand me the little bottle behind it." It's a bottle of Mountain Dew. *Who hides green soda in the laundry room?*

She takes a swig and hands it to me. "Thank you," I utter again, still not quite sure how to react to this woman. Her forceful nature is evident just by being in her presence. Plus, she's a mum of four boys and married to Booth Senior. You need a strong constitution to put up with all those men. She nods and signals with her hand that I'm to share the drink.

I take a gulp and choke on the fiery liquid that sinks down my throat. It's bourbon. Strong bourbon. She laughs. "The only thing that gets me through these parties without shouting a curse word or two myself." She sits on the dryer next to me. "You're a Brit, right? I lived in London for a year after high school. Girls around here don't normally do things like that, but my daddy had a cousin there, and he wanted me to see the world — my daddy, not my cousin."

"I am."

"I always admired British girls. You've got spunk. I had such the best time in that place, got myself a handsome boyfriend from Bristol, learned a thing or two about how to handle my liquor." She takes another swig. She's definitely handling it.

"I thought people around here didn't drink."

"They don't drink in public. If I had a quarter for every woman in this town who has a bottle of liquor hidden in her laundry room, I'd be rich by now. Heck, I am rich. I'd be even richer." She laughs at her own joke and takes *another* swig.

Who *is* this woman? She certainly isn't the Theresa I've seen outside. Her self-assurance unnerves me. She has not a single fuck left to give.

She hands me back my shoe. I go to say thank you but those are the only words that have come out of my mouth since we got here. "Just like new," I say, inspecting it and smiling. I pop it back onto my foot and we get up to leave, but she grabs my arm again.

"A piece of advice. Don't go messin' with the boys around here. People in this town don't take lightly to strangers. And, if the worst happens and you end up pregnant…" She pauses for a final swig, carefully undoing the lid, then screwing it tightly back on again. Is she worried about the smell of alcohol in the air? She should be more worried about her breath, which is strong enough to have me believing that this isn't her first trip to the laundry room this afternoon. "And being forced into marriage, you don't want to be sneaking bourbon in a back room just to get through the afternoon. You understand?" I nod, like a child. She throws on the same perfect, winning smile that she had when I arrived. "Good. Let's go celebrate my boy signing up for a lifetime of dull sex, shall we?"

My conscience gets the better of me. "Surely choice comes into it. I'm not talking about me. In today's world, women don't have to get married if they're pregnant. Surely it doesn't *have* to be that way."

She cups my chin with her perfect French manicure. "Oh, you are such a darlin', aren't you?" she drawls. "Thinking that the women in this town have a choice. The only choice is which Booth we want to marry — preferably one foolish enough to think that *he's* in charge." She lets out a wry laugh and takes her leave.

Eli's mom is a conundrum. She's bitter and twisted but makes it classy. I don't want to be her when I grow up. I want my bourbon in a glass with ice, but I respect, in some small way, her strength of character, considering the life she feels obliged to live — even if most of her courage does come from a bottle.

Somewhere in this house there's a well-thumbed copy of *The Handmaid's Tale*. I'd bet my life on it.

I go back out into the party with a certain confidence. I'd assumed that the people around me were leading perfect, healthy lives. All the while they're keeping their dirty little secrets to themselves.

My own dirty little secret doesn't feel so bad now. In fact, if the occasion arises again, I might be inclined to do more than kiss Eli. If he is truly destined to an unhappily married life, I'd quite like to be the person he dreams of when he closes his eyes at night.

A shiver runs down my spine. What is wrong with me? Maybe that bourbon was a little stronger than I thought. I'd taken a mighty gulp or two before realizing what I was drinking. I should probably avoid Eli altogether, before I do something I'll regret.

Mackenzie and Raylyn are busy setting up on a makeshift stage. The happy couple are supposed to play games to see how well they know each other, that kind of thing.

I can't imagine if we did this back home every time anybody started dating.

'How did you meet Tom?'

'Well, my boyfriend dumped me, so my friends got me drunk and I ended up snogging him on the dance floor at two a.m. Then I went back to his place, shagged him, and it sort of took off from there.'

It wouldn't quite merit a fancy party with games and pie.

"Can I help you guys?" I ask the girls.

"Milly, you made it. Oh wow, so good to see you." They go in for the hug as if they haven't seen me for weeks. It's a great feeling to be part of their little gang. "We're pretty much finished, actually."

Anna-Mae arrives, brandishing the prettiest bracelet. It's a courting gift from Evan. Apart from Jake, I've yet to see any of the brothers at the party. "Where's the lucky guy?"

"Oh, he's here somewhere." She looks around. "He and his brothers are going to sing something, and they wanted to get in a bit of practice beforehand. They used to have a band when they were kids. Haven't performed together in forever."

"Really? That's awesome," I reply. "Eli has such a beautiful voice."

"You've heard him sing?" asks Mackenzie. "He never sings for anybody—well, except for today, but that's because it's special." The entire group stares at me with intense confusion. *Crap.*

A raging blush rises in my normally pale cheeks and I stammer my reply. "I...uh... In... Uh, the coffee shop, the other day I heard him singing along to the radio."

Evan arrives, guitar in hand, saving me from saying anything else that I really shouldn't. I back away, straight onto Eli's foot. He cries out in pain as I stumble and fumble to get away. He reaches out to steady me, gripping my elbows.

"It's okay, Milly. I've got you," he says, making it a million times worse.

Everybody is standing there looking at me trying to stop myself from falling all over him, as he is trying desperately to hold me up.

I have to get away.

I spin around and walk straight into him as he sidesteps in the same direction as me. "Nope," I cry, rushing off in the direction of the house to find the nearest bathroom to hide in.

My knowledge of the vast Booth household is limited, so I go for what I know, ending up back in the laundry room. The last dregs of a bottle of special Mountain Dew are very tempting right now. I resist it. I don't fancy ending up like Theresa.

There's a knock on the door. "Milly," whispers Eli, loudly. The handle turns.

Crap. The last thing I need is someone finding the two of us alone here.

"Go away." A little piece of me gets all fuzzy at the idea that he chased after me. I don't want him to go away at all.

The door cracks open and he peers inside. He has brows knotted so tightly that it looks like it hurts. He's genuinely worried. The confident guy I met the first time I came here is gone.

Shit. I broke him with my lips.

"What is with you?" He walks in and shuts the door behind him, strutting over toward where I'm sitting on my favorite washing machine.

I kick out a leg to keep him at bay. "You shouldn't be here." Today, Eli, in an attempt to send my underwear plummeting to the ground, opted for the sexiest plaid shirt—enough buttons undone to reveal a mere hint of the tautest chest—and button-up jeans that look like they were molded for his pert behind. It's hard to concentrate on sending him away when my brain is urging me to unbutton everything really, really slowly.

He grins. "Why? This is my house."

"I mean in here, with me. I can't be trusted. I already told the girls you sang for me, by accident. Plus your mum..."

"My mama?" His lips twitch. "What's Mama got to do with this?"

"She told me to stay away from the boys here, not you in particular. I don't want to stay away from you..." I bring my knees up to my chest, rolling myself into an impenetrable ball.

His shoulders relax and he takes another step forward. "Oh yeah?"

"No. no, no, no. You stay where you are. That's the problem. You're there with your curls and your butt and your tongue, and I'm going to get pregnant and have to drink bourbon Mountain Dew and glue my feet to the floor."

He tips his head to the side. "Milly, you aren't making a lick of sense." I get up and brush past him, but he sticks his hand out, gently barring the way. "I would never make you do anything you didn't want to do."

"I know. That's the problem. I want to do *you*." I rush out of there and to my car. Two gulps of bourbon half an hour ago hasn't taken me over the limit, but I drive the Pontiac so slowly back to Sal and Carrie's house that I could probably get arrested for going too much *under* the speed limit.

"You're back early," says Sal as I saunter in, miserably, throwing the keys into the bowl by the door. "Something wrong?" I burst into tears and fall into her arms, wiping snotty wet tears all over her shoulder.

"Let me guess," says Carrie from the top of the stairway. "One of the Booth boys."

Chapter Ten

Milly

"My first dalliance with a Booth almost got me thrown out of this damn town," says Carrie from her perch at the top of the staircase.

"Go to bed, but get comfortable, because I have to hear all about this," replies Sal, shooing her hand at Carrie. I release my grip on her and we climb the stairs, eager to hear what Miss Carrie has to say about the most prominent family in town.

She is sitting comfortably, at least four pillows stacked up behind her frail body. We climb onto the bed next to her and she begins. "Back when I was still convinced that I would marry Brad Pitt and move to Hollywood—" Sal does a snort giggle. She looks nothing like Brad Pitt. "If I may continue. There were seven kids in the Booth family. Three sisters and four brothers. Those boys were as handsome as their daddy, and didn't they know it. If you went to a party and the

Booth boys were coming, you knew it was going to be a good night."

"So did people drink and party back then?" I would have thought it was even stricter back when Carrie was young.

She shakes her head, laughing. "Lord no, not officially, but we had some illicit fun. A little liquor, a sneaky kiss or two." Carrie is so pretty. I can imagine her as a sixteen-year-old, with her wild curls and her gorgeous smile. "You've got to understand this town is a little different. A while back — like a long while back, when this town was founded — the people who set up home here had very strict rules about how they wanted to live. Things changed over the years, but the Booths, they kept up those strict rules, convinced everybody that drinking — and sex — were bad. Other families moved on, the population changed, but those rules? They stuck, and as long as the Booths are in charge, they aren't fixin' to change."

"Wow, I thought it was an American thing."

"Oh, honey, I'm not saying there aren't other places around here where they encourage a purer lifestyle, but America is vast and vastly different." She stops to catch her breath. "So Mark —"

"Eli's dad?" I blurt out, gasping as I realize I have exposed myself, like the smitten fool that I am.

Carrie raises her eyebrows and tips her head. "If you'll let me finish, please."

"Sorry," I reply, zipping up my lips with my fingers.

"Mark was one of the wildest. His sweetheart, Theresa, had gone off to London for a year, and he was feeling a little lonely." She reaches under the bed and pulls out the dustiest old suitcase, much to Sal's disgust. "Wait! I have a photo."

She hands us a blurry photo of her and Mark and a bunch of other friends. Eli and his brothers really do take after their father, especially Kyle. My heart sinks. I know this story isn't going to end well.

Turning to me and taking my hands in hers, she says, "Mark took my first kiss, and a lot more from me, and he broke my heart. My daddy was furious, insistin' that Mark marry me, but his parents were having none of that. I wasn't good enough for their boy. They blamed me for sleepin' with him. Can you imagine? I mean, that was the worse forty seconds of my life." She chuckles at her own joke, her whole body shaking with laughter. This brings on a coughing fit that lasts several minutes.

"Do you want us to leave? We can hear the rest later." asks Sal, wringing her hands through lack of any way to help.

"No, honey, I'm fine, really," replies Carrie, as her breathing calms. She puts a reassuring hand over Sal's white knuckles. "So, I had terrible sex, got dumped, then my daddy started feuding with the Booths. All the while, Mark Booth is hailed as the terrible victim of a seductive whore and runs straight back into the arms of his beloved."

"What the fuck?" I'm outraged for her. "Sorry. I didn't mean to swear."

"Oh no, honey," says Carrie. "This absolutely deserves a curse or two. The Booths decided to take it out on my family. They boycotted our store, and nobody spoke to us — not a soul, not even my mother's closest friends. Eventually I went to church, prayed on it and I started apologizing."

"What?" I swallow back my anger. "Sorry. Sorry, go on."

"I stood up in church and cried, *'I have sinned. Lord, forgive me'*."

"In front of everybody?" asks Sal, her eyes wide. "No way!"

Carrie cringes. "Oh yeah. It was real dramatic, arms splayed out, a tear in my eye." She giggles again. I'm glad she finds it funny now. I'd still be fuming all these years later. "Then I went to see all of them, one by one, to apologize for my behavior. People started coming back into the shop, and my mom's friends started coming around again. I left town shortly after."

"But you came back."

She purses her lips. "I came back a changed woman." Her fingers are tightly gripping Sal's hand. "And I came back with the love of my life. My daddy was sick, my grandma was gone and I needed to run the business. I was old enough to know how to deal with people like the Booths, which is to say stayin' as far away from them as I humanly can."

She raises her eyebrows once more and gives me a look that suggests I do the same. "It's not the same thing," I opine. "Eli is different. He's sweet and he's not like his family."

"Honey, he is a Booth. He will tell you that you are the love of his life, and he will break your heart."

"It's not like that," I reply, trying to convince myself that I am nothing like Carrie. "I'm older than you were, and I'm the one with experience, not him. I've slept with several men." My aunties look at each other and back at me. "I am careful. I just don't have the settling-down gene that seems to be so rampant in this family."

"So what were all those tears about, then?" asks Sal, a condescending smile on her lips.

"Uh… Well, I don't know. All right, maybe I caught feelings for this guy. He…uh… He kissed me, his first-ever kiss." I touch my lips as I say it, then throw my hand back into my lap, hoping neither of them noticed. "I'm getting all kinds of emotional, and I'm not sure what to do."

"Sweetheart, you need to stay away from that boy," warns Carrie. "Mark my words… This can only end badly."

She's right. I know she's right. So why do I still want his lips on mine? Why is my stomach doing that swirly-whirly thing at the mere idea of him in those tight jeans today?

Ugh. It's not normal for me to get so hung up on a guy. Not normal at all.

Chapter Eleven

Eli

I walk back out to the party. I'd hoped to sing for Milly today. I thought I'd spot her in the crowd, give her a wink, get a little bit country. Last time I did it, it earned me the sweetest kiss.

"I want to do you." You can't just drop a piece of information like that, then up and leave. What am I supposed to do with that?

Like it's nothing.

Like it's not what runs exactly through my mind every time her hand brushes past mine or she flicks her hair and looks my way.

Like I can't sleep at night imagining how it would feel to take her in my arms and... Damn, I'm way too horny for her to just go slinging phrases like that around.

I pick up my guitar. It's not the same without her in the crowd. My family doesn't appreciate my singing.

My friends are supportive but not like she would be. She would have danced for me.

"You okay?" asks Evan.

I flash him a smile. This is his big day — well, the first of many big days he's going to have this year. I guess I'm singing for him, too.

Fuck. I can't stop thinking about her, and it's driving me wild.

* * * *

It's been a great party and a heck of a day, but as I pick up the mess that our guests left behind, I'm starting to wish that I'd walked out of this house when Milly did. Forty-five minutes ago my mouth lost contact with my brain for a second, and before I knew it, I was spilling my heart out to Mama. That mistake has cost me three quarters of an hour of my life I'll never get back. I love my mother, but what she makes up for in enthusiasm, she lacks in any kind of sensible guidance. I didn't tell her everything — I don't have a death wish — but I told her I was having troubles of the heart, and that was enough to send her down a rabbit hole of terrible advice. And she's still talking.

"So, like I said, life is about getting married and having babies. That's why we we're put here on this goddamn earth after all," she says, with a wink. She enunciates 'goddamn' without actually pronouncing the word. "Honey, if she's not wife and mother material, she's not for you."

The life drains out of me as I nod in total *dis*agreement. "Mm-hmm." *What about love? What about traveling the world? Why does it always have to be* their *way?*

She hands me a soggy paper plate. I'm on trash duty again. Normally we get out the party china for Sunday lunch, but Mama said she didn't want Anna-Mae's family and "*lord knows who they've invited*" breaking her nice plates.

I watch her as she stumbles away, tripping on the step as she goes into the house. She's been drinking again.

Who could blame her? My daddy didn't even wait until the end of the party before skulking off to "*work*." The only thing he's going to be working on until the early hours is Missy Harris.

Theresa and Mark Booth are everything that's wrong with this town. And they have the damned cheek to tell me that I'm supposed to stay 'pure' and 'good'.

Fuck them.

The minute Mama falls asleep I'm out of here. Evan is at The Clearing with everybody else. Nobody's going to even know where I've gone. I've got to be careful. Milly's aunties are back and, from what I can tell, they're not a fan of my family.

Doesn't stop them from coming over every few weeks, eating my Mama's food and pretending we're all best friends.

The adults in this town don't make a damned lick of sense, and I'm supposed to be one of them. I'm expected to just come back from college and fit right in to this meaningless world, where someone fixed the rules a million years ago and nothing has ever changed.

All I want to do is sing for Milly Parker so she'll kiss me again.

And I kind of want to do her, too.

* * * *

Milly

"Milly!" Sal is slumped in my doorway, her arms crossed.

I lift my sleepy head from my computer keyboard, lower down the screen—which really wants to know if I'm still watching—and blink a couple of times to wake myself up. "I'm awake. I'm awake. Is it morning? Did I forget to sleep again?"

"There's a boy outside throwing pebbles at my window, and I'm pretty sure he's not here for either me or Carrie."

What the fuck? "Huh?" *Oh shit, Eli.* "Sorry, I'll...uh... I'll deal with it."

She leans in as I squeeze past her. "It's over, Milly. We're clear on that, right?"

"Yes, of course. I'm sorry, Sal."

What is Eli doing here? Did he take me literally? I don't want to *actually* do him. Well, I do, but I don't think I could stand the backlash from everybody in this whole town if that information got out. Admittedly, it probably wasn't the wisest move on my part to tell him that I wanted to do him. He most likely knows this. That kiss we had was *heated*. I'm pretty sure, taking into consideration the longest-lasting, hardest boner that ever had the indecency to stick into my side, that *he* wanted to do *me*.

Ugh. I need to stop thinking about who's doing who and just get this man off of my aunts' property before it gets ugly.

I rush down the stairs, grabbing a glimpse of my head as I throw on my trainers. My hair is all stuck up on one side and the keyboard has left a heavy impression on my cheek. Oh well, I'm going to dump him, anyway. No need to look hot. I grab a cardigan and shove it over my pajamas before rushing outside.

"Eli," I whisper, loudly, "what are you doing here?"

He sees me and his face cracks into the biggest smile. "Milly." He looks me up and down, then straight back up to my face. "Are you wearing pajamas?"

"Yes." I walk over to him and place a hand on his shoulder. "That is not my bedroom." He glances up to see Sal's angry face glaring at him.

"Fuck." He purses his lips then looks away. "Look… Can we talk? Just talk, that's all." He peeks back up at Sal. "Somewhere other than here."

"We can go sit in your truck," I reply with a conciliatory smile. I follow him over to his very impressive vehicle. It's all brand new and shiny and clean, nothing like Sal's. The Booths do like to show off their wealth.

We get comfy in the cab, and I wait for him to speak. He hasn't made any effort to touch me or shown any sign of interest in me since he got here. We could just be casual friends and I wouldn't know the difference. Maybe Carrie was right and his interest in me has already faded. My heart sinks a little. Was I really so ready to walk away? Of course not. Look at him, sitting there, his biceps straining to get out of that shirt, that rough stubble enticing the brush of my lips against it. All he needs to do is whisk that cap from his head, and I would be on him, ruffling those curls before he could stop me.

He scratches his chin. "I spoke to my mom."

I wasn't expecting that. "You did?" *Shit.* I hope I haven't started World War III.

He fiddles with the steering wheel, occupying his hands. "I didn't say it was you I liked. I just said that I liked someone who maybe wasn't who she had planned for me."

Great. I'm the only unsuitable woman in a ten-mile radius. His mum would have to be pretty ignorant not to work out who he was talking about. "And?"

"She told me to follow my heart, but she said you'd probably break it."

"Ah, well, she's not wrong. I don't know what your life plan is, but if it involves babies and white picket fences, it isn't going to involve me. Plus, I'm not going to hold hands with you for two years, counting the days until I can sleep with you. I need to try before I buy."

He chuckles, hitting the wheel with the palm of his hand. "Try before you buy. Shit, Milly, that's... something else."

"What? You're just happy to wait until it's too late to find out if you're sexually compatible with someone?"

He shrugs. "I don't even know what that means. Isn't it just sex? I mean..." He thinks about it for a second. "You both work on it and learn and teach each other until it's right. Isn't that how it works? I thought the whole fun of it was developing something beautiful."

I turn, sit myself cross-legged, facing him, and rub my mouth while I try to formulate my reply. "Theoretically, yes, but there's so much more. Look... What do you know about sex? I don't mean the birds and the bees. I mean the intricacies of sexuality — kinks, BDSM, that kind of thing."

From his face, I'm clearly speaking a foreign language. "What?"

"Okay, I'll make it even simpler. What if you marry someone who doesn't like to suck you off? There are women out there who balk at the idea of a penis in their mouth. Do you want to go the rest of your life without ever getting a blow job? Or will you one day meet a woman, maybe through work, who you're pretty sure gives good head and be tempted to cheat on your beautiful wife?"

"Cheat? Never." He shakes his head trying to process what I'm saying. "Do you...?"

"Give good head? Yes. Well, I've never had any complaints." *Oh God.* I hope I don't sound like I just go around giving random blow jobs. "Not like, you know, I've given all that many." The relieved look on his face makes me laugh, although I'm not entirely sure whether it's the former or the latter he's relieved about.

"Well then, *we're* good," he replies, placing a hand on my thigh and giving it a squeeze. I was right. He's just relieved I give head.

I roll my eyes and hand him back his hand, taking my time to let go. "No. Firstly, you're not marrying me, *remember*? Secondly, and most importantly, it's not just about you. What about me? What if you have a tiny co—"

"Nope. Massive." He grins. From what I felt through his jeans the other day when he was on top of me, he's not lying.

"Let me finish. What if you can't make me come? What if you can't please me? What if I need nipple clamps and a butt plug to come? Are you prepared to do all that?" He's giving me that puzzled look again. I may have gone too far. "I don't need nipple clamps or butt plugs. It was just an example. You know what those things are, right?"

He shakes his head. I may have terrified the boy into never wanting to ever have sex, ever in the world, *ever*.

Fantastic, Milly, you went too far and broke him again.

"If I loved her, we would work it out," he mopes, sounding totally unsure of himself.

I place my hand on his, gripping his fingers. "But by the time you're married, it's too late. Even if you love someone, sometimes your differences are too vast. Not just sex. Ambition. Parenting style. There's so much you need to know about the person you're going to spend your life with, and sometimes the only thing that makes you keep trying is the intimacy. When the intimacy dies, there really is no marriage left. You might as well just be friends." I look at his sad little face. "This is only me saying that I wouldn't do this and giving you my reasons why. Maybe I'm wrong. Maybe you and your future wife will be perfectly happy."

"Teach me," he says, perking up a little. "Teach me how to please a woman. Teach me how to be pleased. Show me what I want."

I tighten my grip. He's so sweet and innocent, but I just can't. "Eli, I will break your heart."

"No, because I'll know that it isn't forever. I won't ever ask you to court me. I won't ever expect anything more of you than you are willing to give. Like I said before, Milly, I would never ask you to do anything you didn't want to do."

Carrie's story resonates in my mind. "Nobody can ever know. I mean it. We can't be seen together or hang out together in public other than as friends. I can't have any repercussions on my family. I won't allow it. If this got out, they would never forgive me." I would never forgive myself.

The grin on his face runs ear to ear. Not surprising, he's 'on a promise', as we say back home. "So, you'll do it?"

"Friends with benefits?" That furrowed brow again. "Okay. As long as you swear not to fall in love with me and that you're not just saying all of this because of the whole blow job thing."

"Well, that is kinda hot. Cross my heart, Scout's honor, this is just between you and me and I will do my best not to fall in love with you. But it's going to be hard." He winks at me. Not that word again. He glances around us and sneaks a peck on my lips. "Now get on back in there before your aunts come looking for you. They scare the shit out of me."

And so they should. I turn to leave before that peck on the lips turns into something more serious. "I'm going. I'm going," I reply as he leans over me, opening the door and sending my body into meltdown. He smells like terrible decisions and secret liaisons, and it is divine.

Back in my room I cogitate on what just happened. Much as I'd like to pretend I'm this sexually liberated woman who can have a consensual sexual relationship with a man and know that it won't go any further, it's simply not the case.

I might never have fallen in love, but it doesn't mean it can't happen. It's not entirely out of the realms of possibility, even for me. I've always been happy-go-lucky because it never meant anything. The men knew exactly where they stood. This is different. Eli is... special.

And despite being conscious of that, I said yes. Neither of our lives are going to allow us a happy ever after, so I'll take what I can get—mainly because he hasn't left my mind since I met him and nobody has ever lived in my brain before.

This situation is so fucking confusing. All of it — lying to my aunties, keeping secrets from everybody in the whole damn town, including all my new friends.

There's no doubt in my addled thoughts that a psychologist would have a field day listening to this. My mother's insistence on me settling down with the first man who came along — just like she and almost every other woman in my family had — has to have affected me more than I like to pretend. That has to be clouding my judgment. Right?

That's just the tip of the iceberg, too. Having a sexual relationship with someone who has made a vow of chastity is bad, so bad — and not even 'sexy' bad. What if he's just worked up at the idea of having sex? Is it the frustration talking? Will it mean that he'll have regrets one day or, even worse, that he'll hate me forever for allowing him to do something he should have saved for the love of his life? Questions ping around my brain like a low-budget video game.

What I really need right now is a friend to talk to, but my friends over in the UK are busy going about their day, and nobody replies to my calls.

Fuck it. I'm a grown woman. I can do this, can't I? I'm not so sure.

The familiar beep of my phone signaling an incoming call brings me out of my thoughts. Clearly Eli is having doubts, too.

"You okay?"

No, not really. "Yeah, no. I feel a bit weird about what we talked about."

"Me, too. I looked up nipple clamps and butt plugs."

"Really?" *This guy.*

"Yeah. Did you know about fluffy handcuffs, too? Mind blown. Now I need to work out how to wipe the history on my phone."

"Probably a good idea. You want to meet up tomorrow?"

"Sure. I've got something to show you."

I let out a snort. "Oh yeah?"

"Not like that. Something special."

"Good. I think we need to talk."

We fix a way for him to pick me up after work without anybody seeing us. It's kind of seedy to be sneaking around, but that's the way our worlds have forced us to be.

Pseudo-adults not even adulting in the slightest — except when it comes to the adultest thing of all.

Chapter Twelve

Milly

I'm back in Eli's truck, draped over the middle bit between the seats, my head resting on his thigh as he drives us out of town. My heart is beating out of my chest. I'm terrified that somebody will see me.

"This is so fucking ridiculous."

He reaches down and brushes my hair out of my face. "It's only five minutes out of town. I'm sorry. You're the one who insisted that this was a secret."

My first instinct is to reply *'Because of your dad'*, but he doesn't need to know that his dad is a complete asshole. If he hasn't worked it out already, I'm not going to be the one to break the news to him. I already made him google nipple clamps. Today's goal is to avoid springing anything shocking on him. So far it's going well.

"I know you're right. It's just kind of bumpy down here." He slides his hand under my head and keeps it there. He has really big man hands. He's quite big all around, bulked up and tall — or at least taller than most of the people I've dated before. *Am I dating him?*

"Eli, are we dating?"

"Uh…I don't know. Do you want us to be dating?" My stomach does a little backflip because my gut is secretly a romantic. My body really needs to calm its shit. The way he said it, though…like it could happen, like we're not sneaking off somewhere to make out and that this is a date.

Keep fooling yourself. It's not like that and it never will be.

"It's less sordid than friends with benefits." That just hasn't sat right with me since last night.

His hand grasps me a little tighter. "Do you think of what we're doing as sordid? Milly, you are okay with this, aren't you?"

I nestle into his hand. He is warm and comforting and safe. I trust him implicitly, especially when he says things like that. "Yes." In the light of day and with a lot of thought I am okay — maybe not with the sneaking around, but this doesn't mean that I'm doing anything wrong.

On the contrary, lying there on his lap, his fingers running through my hair, feels like the most right thing in the world.

"We're here. You can get up. Nobody comes out here except me." I sit up straight and look around. We're in some kind of farm. There are a couple of outbuildings and fields with horses in them. "I wanted you to meet my babies."

We climb out and I follow him over to a high wooden fence. He climbs up and whistles, but the horses, having seen us arrive, are already galloping our way. He pulls me up next to him and we sit side-by-side, my hand in his.

Dust rises behind the horses as they slow their approach. They're sleek, graceful. It's like a scene out of a movie. "How many do you have?"

"I've got five quarter horses. Trained them myself. The youngest, Smoky, he's still learning. I thought you might like to see me work with him today."

They rush over toward us and bop and boop their big snorty noses all over Eli, vying for his attention. He laughs and caresses them, pulling horsey snacks out of his pocket and feeding them each a handful.

The widest of grins has formed on my lips and I can't control it. It's stupid and silly and girly, but this is the most adorable thing I've ever seen.

Breathe. There is no purpose to this dating. No endgame. I simply cannot fall in love with this man.

Just because his voice soothes my soul, he's great with animals and he's hot as hell, does not mean that anything is going to come of this? He's a catch, and someday some woman is going to be lucky to have him…just not me.

We climb down and he fetches Smoky, bringing him through to a fenced-off area, where a saddle is waiting on a horizontal wooden stand.

"Do you know how to saddle a horse?" I shake my head. He takes my hand, helps me climb over the fence, and we walk over to Smoky. He's quite a big horse and very muscular. I go to stroke him and he lifts his head, sending me back a couple of paces.

"Teach me how to whisper," I say. "That's what you do, isn't it?"

He laughs. "That's what they call it, but there's not a lot of whispering that goes on. It's more like mutual respect. You start off by learning how horses think, then you use that to your advantage." He taps the side of his head. "You've got to get into their minds."

"So what did I do wrong?"

He takes my hand in his and backs away from Smoky. "You see his eyes? They're on the side of his head. He has a blind spot right there." Eli points to the middle of my nose. "So if you walk straight up to him, he can't see you right."

The confident Eli comes forth as he's telling me all this. He's controlled, at home with himself. He is in his element.

Moving us around to Smoky's side, he walks us forward a few paces. "Horses have their own language. You've got to be the boss, but in a horse way, not a human one that involves whippin' or hurtin' them." He taps on a rope in his hands, basically shooing smoky away, then a second time, so we're walking around the arena with Smoky several steps ahead. "Stop. Now turn around and start walking."

Eli jumps up onto the fence and I continue walking around the arena. "Eli, don't leave me," I mutter through my teeth, but he remains seated.

"I will never let you come to harm," he says, with a reassuring smile.

The warmth of his voice courses through me, making my skin tingle. "Okay." For some reason that I cannot explain, I trust this man entirely.

Smoky's warm breath lands on my shoulder as he follows me around like a lost puppy.

"See?" says Eli. "You made a friend. Give him a pet if you want to. He's done great." I step aside and turn around so he can see me this time and he boops me, just like he did with Eli. I might cry again. Who knew horses gave you all the feels?

He spends the next half an hour riding Smoky around the ring, then takes him back to the field.

I wait patiently, wringing my hands, eager to help. "Do we need to feed them?"

"Nope. I come by every morning to check on them and give them anything they need then. They're good." He takes my hand again. "I brought food. You want a sandwich?"

Eli won't feed the horses but he's always trying to feed me. Do I look too thin or something? "Yes, please."

We wash our hands and go through to the barn where he has set out some straw bales. He lays out a blanket, "because of bugs and mice," he tells me. *Lovely.* Then we sit snuggled up to each other, munching on the food he brought and sharing a bottle of Coke.

"This is nice," I say as I lean into his shoulder.

He pecks his lips onto my forehead, wrapping his arm around me. "Can I ask you a question?"

"Sure, although you just did." This is going to be personal. When people ask if they can ask, it's always personal.

"What do you think of me?"

I sit up, cross-legged, my body facing his. "In what way?"

"Do you respect me? Do you think I'm just some ignorant cowboy?" He looks away, avoiding my gaze.

An uneasy smile forms on my lips. "Did I say or do anything that makes you think I don't respect you?"

"No. No, it just matters to me, how you see me."

Why is he suddenly so insecure? Or did I just not notice before?

I place my hand on his cheek. "I see a kind, gentle soul — when you came and helped me out the other day, for example, and the way you're always checking to see if I'm okay. And with the horses... You're so loving with them." He grins at me, then rolls his eyes a little at my accolades. "And you're smart and funny. You're not exactly worldly, but you've been to college, you know all kinds of things about stuff I'd never even thought about. I respect the hell out of you."

He lifts his face to mine. The blush in his cheeks is kind of cute. "Thank you."

I take his hand and entwine my fingers through his, circling the tips on his palm. "It does feel sometimes like you don't belong here. I don't mean you don't fit in. I just wonder if you can reach your full potential if you spend the rest of your life in this town. But I'm biased. The idea of spending my whole life in the same place terrifies me."

"I get that — for me *and* for you."

"And me?" I ask, not knowing if I want the answer. "Have your feelings changed since you've gotten to know me better?"

"You're so strong, like a tornado that blasted into town."

A tornado, huh? I have no comeback for that.

"I feel like I'd spend the rest of my life bickering with you if you stuck around — and I wouldn't mind one bit. And you care about people. You pretend that you don't, but your heart is so big. Plus, you're so beautiful that you make me want to kiss you all the time, even though I can't."

That's the sweetest thing anybody has said about me. He lifts my hand and kisses my fingers, then pulls me onto his lap, leaning back into the straw. "May I kiss you again, Milly?"

"You don't have to ask every time." I sit astride him, lower my lips onto his and savor the warmth of his tongue as it enters my mouth. Releasing him, I snuggle my mouth into the crux of his neck, planting a trail of kisses down to his chest. I can feel him hardening underneath me and I swirl my hips onto his crotch. His eyes widen with pleasure.

There's something so exhilarating about pleasing a man, especially when that man is Eli. It's such a turn-on to know that I can make him want me with just a touch.

He lifts his hands up and hovers them over my breasts, looking me in the eye, seeking my approval. "Can I touch them?"

This is the moment of truth. From this moment on, anything we do goes over and above just kissing. It might be foolish to ask a sexually frustrated man on whose dick I'm grinding if he's really sure he wants to touch my boobs, but I feel obligated to do so anyway.

"Are you positive you want to do this, with me? You don't want to wait? No regrets?"

He pecks me on the lips. "No regrets."

I move his hands to the buttons on my blouse and he undoes them one by one, exposing my best lacy bra.

I wore my prettiest underwear today. The top even matches the bottom.

His eyes almost pop out of his head. He's like a kid in a candy store. Well, a grown-up kid in a booby store. He's fascinated by them, rubbing his finger along the exposed breast then slipping it under the cup and feeling the very tip of my nipple.

I gasp in pleasure. He looks up, concerned. "Did I hurt you?"

"No, it feels good. Nipples are very sensitive for women. Some men like to lick or nibble on them. It's very pleasurable for the woman." I sound like a documentary.

He bites down hard on his lip as I pull at the cups, releasing my breasts. His mouth is on them before I can breathe. I moan with delight.

How is it possible he's never done this before? The man has a talent for it. He swirls his tongue around the very tip of my nipple, sucks and nibbles before releasing.

He moves his hand up, grabs my other breast, toying with my rock-hard nub between his fingers, before leaning back in and starting all over again.

Minutes pass. He never stops, entranced by my satisfaction. The pressure rises between my legs. No man has ever made me come with breast play, but then no man has ever paid them *so much attention.*

I rub myself against him, tightening my thighs around his, tilting my hips, rocking my clit back and forth, back and forth. The hard bulge of his cock, bursting through his jeans, strokes against my panties. It's too hot, too much for me. "Don't stop. I'm going to come," I whisper, as my arousal builds to its crescendo.

He sucks a little harder and my body gives up. Intense waves rise inside me. I shake and gasp above him, lost in pleasure.

He throws his head back and lets out a strangled moan. *Oh shit.* He's coming, too. I grab at his jeans, desperately trying to get them unbuttoned, but it's too late. The damage is done.

"Fuck!" His jeans are soaked. Twenty-one years of frustration have emptied out into his boxers. *Crap.* It's going to be kind of awkward explaining cum stains when he was supposed to be feeding his horses. His face drops, turning from elation to despair, as if he's disappointed me in some way. "No, it's okay. It doesn't matter, I didn't mean..."

Poor thing, he looks like he wants to shrivel up and die.

I didn't see that coming, no pun intended. Didn't think this through at all. I step back off him and he surveys the damage. It's visible but it doesn't look like he just came in his pants. Okay, it does a little. I try not to let him see me staring at his crotch. He feels bad enough as it is.

Humiliated, he packs up his stuff and heads for his truck. I button myself back up, run after him, reaching out as I catch him up, grabbing his arm. "Sorry," he mutters, still walking, dragging me along behind him.

"No, wait, *no.*" I pull on him, trying to get him to spin around, but the man is twice my size and twice as strong. "Eli Booth, you stop right there and look at me!" I shout. He freezes then turns to face me. "You did nothing wrong. This is my fault. I didn't think that we would get so hot and heavy so quickly. I was worried about your jeans, that's all. I don't care that you came. That's kind of the point of making out."

"You looked so surprised." He turns toward me, loosening my grip on his arm. The devastation in his voice is palpable.

"Of course I did. It's customary to tell your partner when you're going to come. I thought you knew, but now I realize as I'm saying it that that's the kind of thing I should have mentioned before we started." I release my grip on his arm and he wraps his hands around my waist. "Was it good?" I ask. "Tell me it was good, at least."

"Oh, fuck, Milly, it was awesome. I had no idea. Man, when you were rubbing on me it was like, fuck, I can't explain it. Good. *Real* good."

"Well then, there's no need to apologize is there?" I say, placing my hands either side of his neck and bringing his mouth to mine.

He kisses me, just a quick peck. "And you?"

"It was wild. The things you can do with your tongue. You're a natural. You sure that was your first time?" I wink at him. "Seriously, *so* hot."

He looks at me, his eyes sparkling, his smile beaming, and we climb into his fancy truck. "I didn't know women came like that. I thought it was more like screaming and yelling. I didn't know your body *moved*."

"It's like sitting on a washing machine during the spin cycle, sometimes your whole body shakes with pleasure and sometimes it's just your core."

"I want to see that," he replies, still grinning like an idiot. His eagerness makes me chuckle. *So keen to do and know everything – and get it right.* He's fragile, too, though. Scared of doing something wrong. "So, when can I see you again?"

I shake my head. "Not for a few days. I'm so busy at the café, and I don't want to get Sal's suspicions up. Plus I...um." I hesitate, wondering whether this is too much information for a first date. "I'm due on, as we say in the UK."

"Due on where?"

"No." I giggle. "I mean I'm getting my period." He cringes and makes a face. I tap him lightly on the arm.

"Stop it. I knew I shouldn't have said anything. I'm an absolute misery one week a month—cramps and migraines. It knocks me out. All I can do, when I'm not dragging myself through the workday, is roll up into a tiny ball under my quilt, eat sugar and cry."

He takes his eyes off the road and stares at me for a second. "Holy shit, really? That sucks."

"Concentrate on your driving. Yes, it does, but it also happens to most women around the world every few weeks, so, you know, we just get on with it."

We pull up to the start of town and he gently tips my head into his lap. I stare at his wet patch. Have I put him off completely with my menstruation horror stories? Hey, he was the one who wanted to know all about women, so I'm going to give him the whole nine yards.

That night I manage to slip in without any questions from Sal and Carrie. I invented a new friend, Ellie-Mae. It's not very original but it came to me on the spot when Sal wanted to know where I was going after work.

I'm feeling warm and fuzzy and, dare I say, a tiny bit smitten by my handsome cowboy. And at the very same time, intensely guilty. Sneaking out is for teenagers, not grown women. I'm doing nothing wrong. Why, then, do I feel so bad?

* * * *

Eli

There are days that you want to last forever. You don't want to go to sleep because it will all be over.

And there are days when you just want to roll up into a ball and forget they ever happened.

And there are days like today. Days where the high is so high you're going to remember it for the rest of your life, and you also find yourself driving home with cum on your jeans.

This is so ridiculous. I want to walk down Main Street hand in hand with Milly, showing the world that I am head over heels in love with this girl, and instead, I'm driving her to the parking lot where she hid her truck.

When I was at college, there was this girl I liked. She was in my literature discussion group. She had a fancy hairstyle, all teased and curled. She wore jeans and heavy makeup and had three piercings in her ear. She'd stand up and read passages from classic books, and the sound of her voice as she pronounced each word, the soft movement of her lips, the emphasis that went into each sentence would make my heart explode.

We were closer than I've ever been with any other woman — more than acquaintances, but never alone, never more than friends.

Kyle went to a different school. *He* was studying law, so *he* got to go to a regular college. I got to study humanities at a college that shared the same moral beliefs as us. It was a *blast*.

That girl broke my heart.

She saw the boots and the hat and she saw a cowboy, one she didn't want to be more than just friends with. She called me "*farm boy*," and she laughed when I read my passages out loud, even though she was just as much a Texan as I was.

Maybe I am a farm boy. I smell like horses half the time, that's for sure. Maybe I do come from a small town with rules that don't make sense to people. I don't drink, and I don't go to parties, at least not the ones my brother throws. I didn't do what a lot of my so-called celibate friends were doing behind closed doors at college. I could have, but I'd made a choice.

I can love, and I can learn, and I can be whoever I want to be. Making choices in your life doesn't have to define you. You forge your own path to suit who you want to become.

With Milly, I can take on the world. Not a second when I'm with her do I feel unloved, disrespected or anyone else other than exactly who I am.

There's something about a person who is so different from you in every way, who doesn't try to change you. Not once has she wanted to mold me into someone she wants. She accepts me for the man I am.

That's all I need, because I know that's all she can give me right now.

It's hypocritical of me to want to change her, so I won't—even though my heart is begging for more.

When she waltzes out of my life, just as quickly as she waltzed in, I'll do my damnedest to understand.

She's going to break my heart, just like my mama said she would, but I'll understand.

In the meantime, I have some googling to do. *Menstruation*. Now there's a thing I didn't realize I needed to know about.

Chapter Thirteen

Milly

Two days later, as predicted by the app on my phone, and, more noticeably my clockwork-precise body, I get my period.

Sal gives me a few days off. I've been working solidly and she's hired another barista to train to help me out when she's not there. With my comfiest pajamas on, I move into my bed with the firm intention of staying there. Netflix and refined sugar are my best friends. There is a distinct possibility that my luxury quilt palace has now become my forever home.

Carrie is up and about. She's feeling better, able to walk around, and she's already raring to get back to work, the complete opposite of just a few days ago. Brave is not a strong enough word for that woman.

On the second day I'm woken from one of my daily naps by a video-call on my phone. I peer into the screen from the darkness of my hovel.

"Hey, you." My heart does a mini leap at the sight of him.

That excited grin on his face when he sees me fills my heart with joy. Surprisingly, he isn't horrified by my grungy appearance. The guy has it bad. "Hi. You weren't at the coffee shop today." His horses boop the back of his head and peer over his shoulder as he talks to me.

I sit straight up, releasing myself from my comfort cave. "You went to the coffee shop? You didn't ask for me or anything?"

"Milly…" He sounds kind of insulted. "I went there with Kyle and Jake. It'd be weird if I *didn't* go."

"Yes, sorry. You're right. I, uh, I didn't think about it that way. No, I'm home. Sal gave me a couple of days off. I'm…sick."

He nods, sagely, as if he knows exactly what I'm talking about and perches himself on a fence. "Lower back pain, headaches, bloating?"

I stifle a giggle. "Have you been on Google again?"

He looks away from the camera. "Maybe," he mutters.

His commitment to the cause is admirable. "Yes, all that and more. I'm not someone anybody would want to be around right now."

"I want to be around you. I'd make you hot sweet tea and rub your back."

Oh. My. God. He's officially adorable. "That is the sweetest thing anybody has ever said to me." My eyes well up with tears. I break into an ugly cry, sobbing so hard that I can hardly breathe, and Eli has to wait patiently for me to stop.

"Mood swings?" he says. I sniff, wiping my tears on the back of my sleeve. I have no shame, apparently.

"Well, look… I gotta go, but I wanted to tell you that there's something on your porch for you. Don't ask me how I got it to you. It involved a little bit of lying and a lot of praying."

He blows me a kiss and we sign off. Pulling my quilt over my shoulders like an oversized puffy cape, I shuffle down the stairs and out to the front door. There's a box waiting for me, neatly parceled up. I grab it and shuffle back up to my den. The smell of the room hits me as I walk back in. Today would be a good day to maybe open a window, have a shower and change my pajamas.

I'm not human yet, but I'm trying.

The tape on the box takes some time to figure out but I manage to get it off after ten minutes of using my house key. There's all kinds of wild and wonderful chocolate and candy, enough to feed ten hungry men. I get a sugar rush just from the smell of it. Digging down farther, I find a well-thumbed book, *The Horse Whisperer*. There's an inscription inside, 'With love from Smoky'. My heart is melting as I dig through his thoughtful little care package. There's an adult coloring book and some pencils and a small stuffed bear with a T-shirt that says 'bear hugs'.

I'm officially a bawling mess again.

Right at the bottom, underneath everything else, there's a letter. He wrote me a goddamn love letter. I don't deserve him, I really don't.

It's sweet and thoughtful and perfectly Eli. He tells me how he felt the first time we met, and how he just wanted to crawl away and die the other night—after the whole *'wet patch'* incident—how amazing I am and that dating me is the best decision he has ever made. It's lovely and gushing and filled with everything I need right now. He signs it with just a little heart, no name.

I hide it at the back of my bedside drawer, inside the book, stuff the rest of the things under my quilt and head off for the shower.

This is not how I thought it was going to be with Eli. It was foolish of me to assume we could keep our emotions at bay. I didn't count on the fact that the man himself is a giant teddy bear with the words '*I wuv u*' emblazoned across his chest. On reflection, assuming that this man who has been raised with certain values when it comes to women would be anything other than adorable when it came to loving them was an error of judgment I might grow to regret.

Chapter Fourteen

Milly

We are once again invited to the Booth household for their Sunday lunch. Sal said it was a monthly thing, but it feels like we've been going every week. I'm quite convinced someone in that family likes to torture me.

My brain is telling me that it's a terrible idea and that I should just stay at home, but I want to see Eli and catch up with my new friends. The text chain has been wild with gossip about possible new courtships, so I have to know what that's all about. Plus, Evan and Anna-Mae had their first illicit kiss, if I understand correctly. The messages are cryptic, too many parents and siblings watching over shoulders. I need to know *everything*.

I'm thirteen years old again, texting my friends about kisses with boys, but life with Sal and Carrie isn't exactly bursting with excitement. I'll take all the thrills I can get.

Today has been spent choosing the right dress, doing my makeup and my hair and generally trying to look pretty. This is so unlike me. If I can't have any interaction with Eli, I want him to at least enjoy checking me out a little.

Another really exciting thing about today is that Carrie has decided to join us. She has a fancy wheelchair, but she's going to try to see if walking with a stick will do for today. I've spent all weekend making her beautiful. It's not hard, because she's a natural. She was fretting about the gray streaks running through her thinning hair, so I convinced her to let me color it last night. This morning I even showed her how to use my straightener. The sight of her with long straight hair sticking out from every angle had us both doubled over. Those curls cannot be restrained. Her clothes hang on her, and nothing can hide the bags under eyes or her hollowed cheeks, but she is beautiful, nonetheless.

I help her walk down the stairs like someone on *The Bachelor* while Sal waits at the bottom. There's a lot of tears, hidden by raucous laughter when she hams it up, then Sal hands her a rose she's picked from the garden, and I melt.

Of all the married couples in my family, I have never seen such love as that between Carrie and Sal. They bicker, like everybody who's been with their partner forever, but they never hesitate to show each other, every day, just how much they mean to each other.

Those two are a couple goal.

As the Pontiac draws up at Eli's house, I'm wringing my hands. It's another boiling hot summer day. Sal mistakes my anxiety for sadness at having to see Eli again. "You can still be friends with him, you know."

The guilt on her face, thinking how sad she's made me, only compounds mine for lying to her.

"It's fine, Sal. I'll be courteous. I get it." The image of the wet stain on Eli's jeans flashes into my mind and I find myself blushing furiously. This doesn't bode well.

We walk through to the backyard. The girls are standing in their usual spot. Their clothes are no longer an issue for me — the long skirts, the even longer hair. All I can see are their smiles and the warmth that radiates when they see me. If someone up high is trying to make me feel guilty today, it's working. I have sinned with Eli Booth and nobody knows.

"So, what's the gossip, then? What's all this I hear about new courtships?" They giggle and look around to see if their parents are listening.

"Are you coming to The Clearing again?" Raylyn whispers, loud enough for just us to hear. "We'll talk then."

"Secrets? I love it!" I reply, trying to keep my voice down. "Count me in."

The boys join us. Eli stands at the back. He lets out a little gasp, then composes himself, tilts his head as he checks me out. Yeah, I look *good*.

He's the confident man I first met only a couple of weeks ago — cocky and self-assured, joking around with the lads. The flutter in my tummy every time I get to sneak a glance at him is ridiculous, but I can't help myself. I'm a hapless teenager all over again.

I head for the buffet table — got to find something to distract me from those blue eyes and that damned unruly curl. I'm starving. There's a wide array of weird and wonderful dishes. Salad isn't always salad, sweet and sour takes on a whole new meaning and traditional ingredients are for amateurs. If at least one ingredient didn't come out of a can, then the dish hasn't earned its place on this table.

It's times like this that a glass of chilled white wine would do me the world of good. I settle for water. My body still hasn't acclimatized to the stifling heat. Outdoor events, if they're not in the chill of the evening, exhaust me.

A finger runs its way from my neck down my spine. I freeze. Glancing over my shoulder, I see Eli and smile. No, wait. Kyle. *Ewww*.

He grins. His hand has settled in the crux of my back. *Creepy*. "Hey, Pink."

"Kyle." I try to smile but the disgust on my face must be evident. I shuffle around to get away from his touch.

"What are you doing on your own? A nice girl like you. My mom told me about British girls, warned all us brothers about you." *Did she now? Perfect*. Then again, she's not wrong.

I raise my eyebrows. "Warned? Am I a threat to you, Kyle?"

"She said you might be open to things we're not. You know, us sweet little Booth boys… We have to be careful around girls like you." I gulp back my revulsion at the way I'm being spoken about behind my back. Eli never mentioned this. Then again, he probably knew what my reaction would be.

I glance over at Eli's mom. She's hammered. Now I know about what's hidden in the laundry room, I can't unsee it. She's always hammered. It's just that she hides it really well, one hand on a chair or a table to steady herself, a permanent fake grin on her face, always chewing a stick of gum. How many bottles are hidden around her house? From the look of her, quite a few.

"Best keep far away from me, then," I reply. He's doing his best to get into my personal space and it's harder and harder to back away. My butt hits the edge of the table. Another step back and I'll be wearing Sal's mac and cheese.

I put my plate and cup down behind me. I'm going to need my hands. His finger slips under my chin, and I whack it away. Fire burns in his eyes. Nothing riles a bully up more than a victim who fights back.

How can nobody see this?

Why is nobody helping me?

"Mill-lly." It's Addison. I breathe. She grabs my arms and whisks me out of Kyle's shadow.

"You okay?" she asks through gritted teeth.

"Yeah, he was one move away from losing a testicle."

Her eyes widen and she giggles at my use of a word that has probably never come out of her own mouth. "Milly, you are so *wild*." It's said with respect and a touch of awe.

I chuckle. "No, I'm just like you, promise. Are you coming to The Clearing?"

"Yeah, are you kidding? There's so much to talk about. Mackenzie's big news. I mean it's just, like... I can't talk about it but it is *big*."

I stay with the girls until we head out. I don't want to bump into any member of the Booth household except one. He's never far from us—near enough to reach out and grab him but far enough so the electricity between us doesn't make sparks.

His gaze never leaves me. Did he not see then, when Kyle approached me? Did he not want to save me? I take a look around the garden. The chain of gaze doesn't start with Eli. His father is staring intently at him staring at me. *Crap.* Well, that explains Eli's lack of interaction.

We are being observed.

My heart sinks. I can't come here again. It won't be long before people start to notice. Risking anything getting back to Sal and Carrie would be foolish. If I want to see Eli, in any capacity, it will have to be away from anybody's regard. Seedy just got seedier, our secret more secretive.

Booth Senior catches my eye and stares right back. My heart beats tightly in my chest. *Fuck you and your antiquated patriarchy.* I glare back at him, hard enough to make it very clear that he doesn't scare me.

He looks away. I win this round. Is any of this even worth angering that horrible man? For a love that will never be anything more than behind closed doors.

My glance goes back to Eli. *Yes. One hundred percent.*

Despite being followed around by the local secret service, I decide to go to The Clearing. A chat with the girls sounds like just what I need to get my mind off the fact that Eli is wearing a Henley shirt today.

It's like he did it on purpose, teasing me that way, knowing that I can only look and not touch. *Meh.* I did the same thing to him. If I can get a moment alone with him today, the risk of clothes being ripped from bodies has been elevated to high.

We pile into the car, as usual, and Anna-Mae regales us all with the intricacies of her first kiss with Evan. Now that they're courting, they have decided that they should be allowed to go on private dates, not that there's anywhere truly private in this town. You couldn't get away with snuggling up to your boyfriend in any of the restaurants on Main Street without being observed.

The girls explain that there are no hard and fast rules. You're all allowed to do what you want, but you're just encouraged not to engage in anything sexual before marriage.

The image of Eli's orgasm face saunters into my mind, uninvited. I glance around me. Thank God nobody here can read minds.

"We know what people think. They all think we're emotionless zombies until we've got a ring on our fingers, but it's not the case."

I wouldn't have used the word 'zombies', but I may have judged them too harshly when I arrived. In my head, of course, not to their faces.

"So, what was it like?" I ask. "Was there tongue? Was he any good?"

"It was magical," she replies, going into great detail about how he took her head in his hands and how he went really slowly, making sure she was comfortable with it all. Evan sounds just like his brother. It's a wonder those boys turned out as good as they did with the parents they were given. Kudos to both of them for being so sensitive to their partners' needs.

The entire conversation moves on to kisses in general. I, as their resident sex guru, get asked to describe my best kiss. I close my eyes, feel the firm pressure of Eli's mouth against mine, the warm slick sensation of his tongue as it is slid between my lips, reliving my body's instinctive reaction as he held me to him.

The girls form a hushed silence as I describe in intimate detail how every nerve on my body turned to fire as I succumbed to my mystery lover's kiss.

"We're here," announces our driver, and we are roused from our lustful thoughts.

It will take every willful bone in my body not to run up to Eli and kiss him when we get there. The tiniest part of me wishes that I'd waited patiently and politely until everybody saw what a good, sweet woman I am, and they allowed me to court him.

Almost. Like I said, I won't be sticking around for the whole 'happy ever after' thing. In any of the scenarios I have considered, I always end up breaking his heart— and mine too.

Finally sitting on the grass under the shade of a tree, a few feet from where the boys are playing some kind of wrestling game, the girls start sharing their news.

"So, Luke and I have been talking, and I think we're going to start moving toward a courtship. It's early days, but I am *so* excited," says Addison. The other girls seem to know about this already.

"So, which one is Luke?" I ask. She discreetly points out one of the guys next to us, with a giggle. "So this is like a pre-courtship, right? You're just chatting by text and hanging around a lot, but not on your own." She nods. I'm finally beginning to understand the process.

My gaze stays on Luke, but I catch Eli out of the corner of my eye, staring at me staring at another man. I turn to look at him. My insides haven't quite calmed their ardor from the car conversation and that Henley is doing things to me.

I bite my lip, our gazes lock and we cannot look away.

"Now for Mackenzie's news," says Raylyn, clapping her hands with excitement.

"Spill! I want to know everything," I say, only half in the conversation. The other half of my mind is wondering what else you can do on a blanket, on a hay bale.

Mackenzie takes a deep breath. Her voice is unsteady. "Well, I heard from my sister that someone's daddy contacted my daddy to talk about setting up a courtship."

I turn toward her. She has the widest grin on her face, but her eyes tell a different story. "I thought you guys chose your own partners."

"Well," she answers, "sometimes we do and sometimes, when someone is a little shy, our parents help give us a nudge in the right direction. We still get to say no."

This is a lot to take in. "So you can just jump into a courtship with someone you've never even considered before, without even talking first? Okay." *Good God*, I can't even imagine who my mother would have chosen for me. "But courting is a big commitment, not to be taken lightly."

Mackenzie shrugs her shoulders. The girl wants her first kiss, and she wants it *now*.

"Tell them who it is. Tell them who it is," says Raylyn, about to burst.

"Well, when my sister told me, I was, like, what if I don't like him, but when I heard who it was, I was so surprised." The boys have stopped wrestling and I can see that those listening in to our conversation are now relaying the information among themselves. She leans right in and whispers, "Eli."

The girls squeal in excitement. "What?" I reply, much louder than is necessary. Everybody turns to look at me. In my panic, I throw on the famous fake smile patented by Eli's mum, adding, "That. Is. Fan-tastic. Oh. My. God. I am *thrilled* for you!"

I do this kind of out of body thing where I am still there but my mind is reeling so much and my heart beating so fast that I'm only really present physically. Grin glued on my otherwise-devastated face, I join the other girls in hugging Mackenzie.

I knew this would happen, but he's supposed to fall in love with someone after I had already left. Not now. I'm not ready.

It's selfish and childish of me to want to have Eli to myself until I'm ready to give him up, but that was the deal. He wanted that, too, didn't he? It was his damn idea.

I turn to look over at him, but the guys are patting him on the back and congratulating him. In his defense, he looks as dumbstruck as I am right now.

Fuck. Fukkity fuck. I want to get up. I want to leave, go hide in the forest somewhere and weep, but I have to sit through another twenty minutes of girl talk, mainly involving this budding new relationship.

"He's like the most eligible bachelor in town," says Raylyn. "You are going to have such a massive wedding." This opens the conversation up about wedding dresses and rings and all kinds of things that these girls have dreamed of their whole lives — the big house, the fancy cars, everything that comes from a good husband who works hard. That's the gist of what the women in front of me dream of living one day.

I'm tending toward being judgmental again.

If I do ever tie the knot, it'll be a quick affair — in and out and off on a honeymoon. Whichever country my husband and I haven't already visited will be our destination. The only difference will be a ring on my finger.

Eventually, Anna-Mae and Addison decide to go chat with their men, and Mackenzie makes a tentative move toward Eli. The group disperses. I sit there, alone, running my fingers along the dusty ground, ruing the day I ever set eyes on that man.

Mackenzie sits next to him. Her face is filled with promises and wishes. This is what she wants. She's bagged a Booth, and a handsome one at that. He works for his dad. I've never quite worked out what he does, but he must have a decent amount of money in his bank account—enough for a home and kids, and a stay-at-home wife.

The ridiculousness of the fact that it never once occurred to me that he was such a good catch, financially, makes me chuckle. I only ever saw his personality. Okay, I might have been taken a little by his looks, too. He could have rolled up in a rickety old banger and I wouldn't have batted an eyelid.

If you're not looking for forever, then you're not looking for financial stability and whatever that might bring. You look for the joy that that person brings you now. Every man I have ever dated has brought me joy, until he didn't, and that was when I said goodbye. I've seen how marriage dulls the senses, and how ordinary everyday life makes you a shell of your former self.

I am *not* that person.

My laughter hides my pain. A little teeny-tiny part of me wonders what their house will look like. Will she get dressed up one day and waltz down the stairs, like Carrie did, with Eli waiting at the bottom with a rose? Will he rub her back and make her hot sweet tea? Tears sting my eyes and I let them fall as I sit not ten feet from the man I thought was mine and the woman who will be his wife.

My stupid heart is splitting in two.

A heart I didn't even know could be broken.

Seeing me sitting alone, wallowing in my misery, Raylyn, convinced that I'm just miserable seeing all these happy couples, first tries to comfort me, then offers to drive me home.

Our gazes haven't crossed once, despite my efforts, and he has made no attempt at communication. My phone remains silent.

I try to explain all this to myself, reasoning with logic so evident that it hurts my brain. I fail miserably. None of this makes sense.

I knew this would happen. I knew that the minute his parents got a whiff of any involvement between us it would be stopped short.

And yet, for some reason, I thought we could get away with it. My mind decided for me that it totally didn't matter that I was falling in love with him, knowing full well that it would.

It is his turn to break me.

Chapter Fifteen

Eli

Fuck.

"Mama..." I whine down the phone. I want to add *'what the fuck?'* but I don't fancy getting my ass kicked when I go home. "Why did you let him do it?"

"It's for the best. Mackenzie is the sweetest girl. She'll make a good wife."

The best for who, exactly? Not for me. Neither of them has ever wanted what was best for me. They're two of the most selfish people you could ever meet. Not once have my parents ever done what was best for any of their children.

"I don't want a good wife. I don't want a wife at all."

She *tuts* and emits a large sigh down the phone. "Now don't be silly, honey. Of course you do. That big old house of yours is sitting all empty, waiting for the right woman to come along and fill it with babies."

Does she even believe what she's saying? She had four boys and acts like she regrets every second of it. We're an inconvenience at best, when she's not putting on her airs and graces for her guests.

"Eli," says a gruff voice. My father is in the building.

"Yes."

"Don't go upsetting your mama like that. We did what's best for you. A man your age and you haven't even looked at a woman since you came back from college."

Oh my God. Did they seriously think I would come back here and jump into a relationship with the first girl I see? "It's been a month, and I *have* – "

"A suitable woman, not some pop princess from thousands of miles away with pink hair and tattoos." *She has tattoos? Holy shit, I need to investigate that further.* Daddy dearest has been googling, too. "Eli, it's time to man up. Take responsibility. This is the right thing to do, and you know it – get down to working hard, setting up a nice little family in your home and forgetting about all this nonsense with your singing."

My cries are falling on deaf ears. They don't care. They just want to get me married off to a '*respectable*' bride and out of their home. I hang up and switch off the ringer on my phone.

I need to talk to Milly about this but she's nowhere to be seen. Fuck. I can't believe I'm a grown man and my parents are fucking up my whole life because they don't like the look of someone's hair.

She could be a virgin. Perfect wife material. She's not – she told me as much – but they don't know that. They can't see past their antiquated ideas.

Mackenzie is waiting for me. She taps the grass next to her. She dresses and does her hair like people in this town expect from girls her age.

And yet she might not be a virgin, either. It's not like it's written on your face.

I take a few calming breaths and sit down beside her. Might as well make them all think that their plan is working while I work out one of my own.

"Mackenzie," I say. "Does nobody ever call you Mack? Or Kenzie?"

"No, just Mackenzie."

It's so formal. Too many syllables for everyday life. I'm being picky with her, trying to find fault. She could be perfect and she wouldn't be enough.

"What do you like to do, Mackenzie, in your spare time?"

"I like to paper craft—you know, make little cards and letterheads and stuff. I ride, too. You've got horses, don't you? I *love* horses." I try to feign interest, but all I can hear is Milly's voice saying, *"I've ridden,"* and knowing that wasn't what she'd meant at all. Mackenzie's voice drops and she looks down at her hands. "You don't have to—you know—if you don't want to. I totally get it. I thought I was in love once. He, uh…he was really sweet to me, but it turned out that he was really sweet to all the girls. If there's someone else you like…" She's rambling, poor girl. None of this is her fault.

"I'm not sure. I don't know." I am and I do. "I need time."

"Take it." She puts her hand on my knee. "I'll be here when you're ready."

Mackenzie is such a sweet girl, and she does *love* horses, I guess, so she's got that going for her. If there was no Milly, maybe I'd have given Mackenzie a chance. Then again, I've known Mackenzie for a while, and I've never looked twice at her.

There is only one woman who caught my eye and made me hitch my breath the first time I saw her. She's the one who holds my heart.

Fuck.

* * * *

Milly

I wait for my sadness to turn to resilience, just like it's done every other time a boy has moved on from me, but this time it doesn't come. Maybe it's because I'm far from my home and my friends or maybe because our unique situation is such that I really do care after all.

I don't want to. I want to be worry-free just like when I arrived. I hate myself for being so soft. This proves the point that I always make. Love isn't worth it. Either you turn into a married zombie or it breaks your heart.

Home is just a solitary as The Clearing. Sal is doing inventory at the shop and Carrie is sleeping. It's not like I could confide in them, anyway. Grabbing the keys to the truck, I leave a Post-it at the door *'Gone out with friends. Don't wait up'*, and go to the only place around here I'm guaranteed not to bump into anybody.

Not tonight anyway. Eli is busy with other things.

My favorite horse friend in the whole world — admittedly my only horse friend in the whole word — is happy to see me. He gives me boops and snorts, but he really wants treats. They're kept in an old office at the back of the barn with a desk and a couple of white boards. Now it's just a dusty room filled with horse treats, vitamins and tack. The smell is overwhelming. Eli really needs to give this place a damn good clean out.

A truck draws up as I'm scooping up the treats. Can they see my car? It's parked behind the barn, so as not to draw attention to my presence there. Explaining that would be a bit tricky if any of the Booths decide to pop by. Looks like I made the right choice.

I push a tub of treats out of the way and crouch down under the desk. The thick dust stains my pretty summer dress. Why the fuck aren't jeans a thing for woman here? That's it. Tomorrow I wear shorts, damn it.

I peek out from my hiding space, to see who it is. Eli. My heart skips a beat. Did he follow me here? No. He's just outside on the straw bales, and he's not alone.

Wow.

He couldn't wait to show Mackenzie everything he's learned, could he? The two of them mess around, play-fighting. I can hear her giggles as he pulls her down onto the straw bales and makes out with her. The sound of kissing soon becomes the sound of lovemaking, and I am forced to hear every sordid little detail. The gasps the moans, the search for a condom in a wallet. Everything is played out just feet away from where I'm sitting.

The fact that he has condoms on him tells me everything I need to know. I'm an idiot. He must be laughing at me behind my back.

It's a total of twenty-seven minutes from arriving until they finish in a glorious, ecstatic chorus of yeehaws—an admirable achievement for his supposed first time. The sadness envelops me. Tears run down my cheeks, and I don't bother to wipe them. They plop onto the dusty floor forming dark little spots. The anger, too. How can he be so blasé with her, so happy to just jump right in, when he'd convinced me of his so-called vow of chastity? I've been such a fool.

My phone beeps and I stick it on vibrate. I do not want him knowing I'm here. I've been humiliated enough. It's Eli. Calling to tell me all about it? Ugh. I don't reply but he calls again.

"Where are you? Did you leave?"

"As if you care."

"Milly." His exasperated tone is clear.

I wipe a tear from my cheek with my dusty fingers. "Leave me alone."

"Seriously, where are you? I want to talk."

"You do not want to know. Trust me."

"I don't even know what that means. I told Mackenzie I wasn't ready for a courtship. I'm not. I'm dating someone else…someone I care about."

I shifted around, the squatting hurting my legs. Should I just reveal myself, get it over with? "Liar. I know that's not true."

"Look… I'm at The Clearing. Just tell me where to find you and I can explain everything."

What the fuck? I peeped up. "You're not in your barn?"

"No. What—?"

I stick my nose up again, but I can't see them. "Who the hell just fucked in your barn, then?"

"What? Are you there? I'm on my way."

It takes Eli half an hour to get to the barn. Thirty minutes of having to listen to two perfect strangers make out, loudly, again. Whoever this man is he has the stamina of an ox. Not twenty minutes after he's finished, he's raring to go again.

Eli's truck roars into the car park and I pop my head up to see what's about to go down. He walks out of the dust cloud like a fucking avenger. "Kyle, get your naked ass out of my barn."

Kyle. Of course. I *am* an idiot and should have worked that one out straight away. That wasn't the work of a virgin. He might be a complete and utter dickhead, but that man has not missed out on the woman-pleasing gene. At least, I'm assuming that's the case. I wouldn't put it past any woman who finds herself in bed with him to fake it. He's definitely the kind of guy who won't accept that he's anything less than amazing under the sheets.

There's shouting and the sound of a tussle. Giggly woman stands between them, trying to calm them both down. I climb back under the desk before anybody sees me. Kyle scares the shit out of me. I don't want to give him any more ammunition against me. He is his father's son, and I don't fancy being chased out of town like my auntie was.

Face to face I've held my ground, but my throat tightens at the idea that he finds out I'm here and that I told Eli. His revenge would be brutal. The tone heightens and my hands begin to shake.

Giggly woman begins to cry, snapping Kyle out of his anger. Maybe her daddy is important. He wouldn't care about some woman unless he had a vested interest. They leave, doors slamming, truck racing off down the road.

"Milly!" shouts Eli, from inside the barn. "You here?"

"Under the desk." He runs into the room and crouches down next to me. "Is he gone?" He gives me a comforting smile, and I fall into his arms. The overwhelming emotions running through me are too much — hurt, sadness, fear. I'm past crying. I just want to hold him. He lifts me out and carries me over to the straw bales. "Don't let me go," I whisper, as the rough stubble on his cheek rubs against my tear-stained face. "I want to remember this feeling."

"I told her no." His voice is soft, worried.

Leaning back, I stare into his soulful eyes. "You'd be lucky to have her."

His lip trembles. "I want you."

"I want you, too." The absurdity of me even thinking that Eli and I could work out, that I could suddenly become the woman he needs is a symptom of how strong my feelings have become for him.

He takes my head in his hands, crashing his mouth onto mine. He didn't even ask this time. Desire has turned to passion. It's no longer that he wants me. It's need that seemingly drives him. His kiss is hard and forceful. He holds me to his body, his cock, hard and ready. He knows how incredible it feels when I make him come, and he wants more.

I pull away. "This has to be the last time. I might be what you want, but she's your future, not me." He grips me tighter and lets out a little choke. Emotional pain sears through my chest. I'm breaking up with him and he knows it.

He shakes his head, tears forming in his eyes. "No."

I sink my forehead onto his. "I can't do that to Mackenzie, and I can't do that to you."

"No," he repeats, unable to find the right words to make me stay.

"One last night together, just you and me. Tonight. Then we both walk away. No regrets, remember?" I don't believe a single one of the words coming out of my mouth. "And no sex. We can fool around, but you save that for her."

His jaw tightens. "I want it to be with you."

"One day you'll want it to be with her." I give him a half-smile. "I know it."

"It will always be you." His voice cedes defeat. He is going to do as I ask, even if it's not what he wants. "*I'll never make you do anything you don't want to do,*" he'd said, and he'd meant it.

"Is there anywhere we can go, somewhere with a bed? Somewhere special." My mind wanders to the seedy motels featured in TV shows. "Or somewhere private, at least. I don't want Kyle to come back and find us."

"I have just the place," he replies.

Chapter Sixteen

Milly

I leave my truck there and climb up beside him in his. Not a word is uttered as he drives us farther out of town. My hand is in his, but his palms are clammy, his grip weak. We draw up at a home not dissimilar to Sal and Carrie's. Piles of sand and wood are dotted around in the front yard. It looks like a building site.

"Where are we? Are you sure they don't mind?"

"I'm sure." He grins at me. "Welcome to my house."

His *what* now? "You have a house?"

"I bought it last year. My grandparents gave their house to Kyle and left the equivalent in cash to me, Ev and Jake. This is what I bought. It needs some work, especially the inside. A woman's touch."

So this is where I might have lived — if wishes were fairy-tales, Brits weren't harlots and people were allowed to leave this town.

Eli opens the door, puts his phone onto torch and guides us through the dark interior until he finds the fuse-box. A couple of switches clicked and the lights are on. The house is devoid of furniture. Outdated paper peels and droops from the walls. He wasn't kidding about it needing some work.

His breath is nervous, hitched. I place my hand on the small of his back, rubbing it. "Are you excited or scared?"

"Both. Can I be both?"

"You can be whatever you like, but you don't need to be scared." I wink at him. "I'll never make you do anything you don't want to do." This earns me another smile.

"Oh, I want to do everything," he replies, returning my wink.

He pulls me up the stairs. "Hold on." I stumble trying to keep up and he bends down and whisks me into his arms. *Oh, okay.* The man is impatient.

Upstairs is untouched. Old dressers and large wooden wardrobes fill the bedroom. There's a big wooden framed bed, perfectly made up. "The mattress is new. I stay over sometimes when I come here after work. Between the horses and the construction work, it's practical."

He sits on the bed and I stand in front of him, my legs between his, unbuttoning my dress until it tumbles to the ground, his eyes watching it as it goes. "Where can I freshen up?"

His hands brush the outside of my thighs until they rest on my hips. He pulls me to his crotch, his face firmly entrenched between my breasts. "Do you have to?" comes the muffled reply.

"Yes, my hands are all dusty. I just want to wash them. You should, too. Clean hands are important." I grab his hand, inspect it. "And nails, too."

"Where's your tattoo?" he asks, inspecting every inch of me.

I take his hand and place it on my hip. "Here, but you can look at it in more detail *after* you've washed your hands." If ever there was an enticement for Eli to have clean, sanitized hands, my naked, tattooed body was it.

We go through to the master bathroom. I try to wash my hands and forearms, but he's like an octopus, standing behind tracing his fingers all over my body. I tap him away.

"Hey!" he says, pouting.

"Hey, yourself. Wash your hands then come find me." When he walks back into the room I'm under the covers, my underwear and dress neatly folded on a chair.

"Why are you hiding?"

I hand him the corner of the sheet.

He reveals my body, bit by bit, his jaw dropping as he unveils me.

"You look awfully pale. Are you okay?" I swear all the blood in his body just raced to his crotch.

He can't get his clothes off quick enough. I've imagined his body, felt it through and under his clothes, but nothing could prepare me for the beautiful man standing before me.

He is muscular, the body of a man who spends his evenings doing up his home and riding his horses, a worker's body, strong arms, tight thighs. No wonder his jeans fit him like a glove. And he's tan. My English body is so pale it blends with the bedding. He is glowing.

It's going to take every inch of my willpower not to fuck him tonight.

"Last chance to back out. This isn't penetrative sex, but it might as well be. It's as close as you can get. I won't mind. I need to be sure."

He sticks a finger under my chin, brushes his lips across mine. "Thank you for your concern, but I know exactly what I want and it's the person lying next to me in this bed." My heart melts. He is so sexy and so perfect.

Don't fall in love with him. Don't fall in love with him.

"We start with you," I say. "No arguments." I know how easily he comes. I don't want to get him overexcited and ruin it. We have all night. I lift the sheet farther and he joins me, cautiously. "You can say no. You can stop at any moment." We are face to face, naked.

"Can I just look at you, touch you?"

"Okay, but not between my legs. We'll save that for later." He acquiesces with a smile.

Taking a deep, deep breath, he runs his fingers up and down my stomach and thighs. It tickles on occasion, and when I giggle, he balks then smiles and carries on.

"I'm ready," he says, rolling onto his back and lying there motionless, hands by his side, as if I'm about to remove his appendix.

His face is picture of excitement. *Christmas in July.* I trail my fingers along the little groove in his abs until I reach his cock. He is unshaven, not even the tiniest trim. It's so rare and I don't mind one bit. He is utterly untouched.

I wrap my fingers around it. His gasp is louder than I imagined it would be, and it makes me giggle. "Wow," he whispers. For the last half an hour his conversation has been reduced to monosyllables and grunts. I'm guessing that means he's enjoying himself.

"You can speak, you know. Tell me what you like and what you don't like." I sink down the bed, parting his legs and getting on my knees in front of him. My hand is still very much grasping him. I lower my mouth onto him and his whole body shudders.

"I like that," he groans. "Fuck, I like that a lot." He leans up on his elbows. "Is this a blow job? Are you sucking me off?" Now he won't shut up.

I lift my mouth off him and smile. "Yes. Now lie back and enjoy it." I find a rhythm, hands and mouth working in unison, and he's quickly ready to come. My efforts to make it last are fruitless. He's too green. Within a couple of minutes, he's writhing beneath me.

I wrap my fingers around his balls, tugging at them ever so gently. "I'm going to... *Ohhhh* fuck!" He releases. I finish him with my hand, watching him as he comes. "*Ohhhh* wow. Oh fuck. Oh Lord."

He takes a minute to get himself together then hoists himself up on to his elbows. "How is that *just* a thing? Like how is that *not* sex? Is sex better than that?" I nod and he flings himself back on the bed, his hand flying to his forehead in disbelief.

"It's just a blow job," I reply. "There's so much more to sex than that. Trust me."

"Not fucking possible." He's bringing out all the swears tonight. "Is it my turn now, to do that to you, to make you come like a washing machine?"

"You make it sound so sexy. Yes, if you'd like." I was pretty turned on, but he's not making it easy to stay that way. "Scuttle down between my legs." I grab some tissues I'd prepared earlier and wipe my hands while he gets into position.

"You're bare."

"Bare? Oh. Yes, women tend to shave or wax their private parts. But you don't have to. Some women aren't aware that they can or should do it—and others just don't want to." He listens, takes it all in. He's going to get five stars at the end of this lesson. I grab his hand and place it on my clit. "This is the most sensitive part of a woman's body. You need to be gentle with it, never rub it when it's dry. This is what makes most women come."

He lifts his finger up and down, taps it a couple of times. "Like this?"

"We'll work on it. You can lick it, too, but we'll get to that in a minute. Next" —I sit up and lower his finger down—"is the vagina. This is where your penis goes." I swirl his finger around the entry. "You see how it's wet. It has to be wet for sex."

"I know how people have sex, Milly. I'm a virgin, not an idiot. I can put my finger in too, though, right? I know that much."

"You can…but be gentle." He explores my core. Entering my vagina, rubbing his finger around my clit, gauging my reactions. "Every woman, ah," I gasp as he swirls around my clit, "likes different things. You need to ask her what she likes. I like to be licked, but I love to be touched. You get the right combination of clitoral and vaginal stimulation, and I will come."

"Whoa, the pressure," he says, sitting back on his knees, rubbing his hands together, and taking in everything I just said. "I can do this, right? Sure, I can. Here goes. You ready? I'm ready. Let's go." This is the most bizarre foreplay I've had in my life, but he's cute and… O*ooooh. My. God.* He's good.

He licks and swirls and caresses. At one point there are two hands and his tongue. I don't quite know how, but it works and it's incredible. He gets a rhythm going and I am his. I shake and shiver under his touch. "Yes… Fuck."

His eyes widen as I come on his fingers. "It's moving."

"I know," I gasp as the orgasm rocks through my body. *I know.*

* * * *

"You have five questions, only five."

He runs his finger between my breasts and around the tip of my nipple. "Well, that's not fair. How can I get to know you with five questions?"

"If you use them wisely, you've got this." I lift my head to sip my glass of water, but it trickles down my chest, to be licked up by a rogue tongue.

"Okay, but you only get five about me, then."

I glance at him. "Mr. Open-Book? Wow, what do I *not* know about you?"

"How many people have you slept with?"

Okay. Straight in there. "Five. The bad boy I lost my virginity to, the homely guy I dated after the bad boy, who turned out to be so boring I almost died, then the first real boyfriend."

He props himself up on one arm. "First love?"

"Is that a question?"

He shrugs. "Maybe."

"I've never been in love."

His eyes widen. "I'm going to swing back to that, but please go on, *ma'am*."

"The terrible decision after the first real boyfriend cheated on me, then the guy I dated at college, who was neither bad nor boring, nor a terrible decision. More…out of my league." I sit up properly and try to drink again. There's no air conditioning in this house, and even with the window open, it's sweltering.

"Nob—"

"Don't say nobody's out of my league, Eli. I might be what some people consider 'famous', but I'm not a top model or a megastar. There's a scale, and I'm kind of around the middle. I'm cool with that." He looks at me with an *I-think-you're-beautiful* smile and I throw back a *you're-just-saying-that-because-I-sucked-your-cock* look.

"What makes someone out of your league?"

I count how many that makes on my fingers. "Is this another question?"

"Jeez, you're tough."

"I'll give you this one for free. It's someone who wears expensive clothing, which he changes every season, who drives the latest car, not necessarily the most expensive, just the one everybody is talking about. His shower gel matches his deodorant, which matches his aftershave, so you only get one distinctive smell. His chin could cut ice. His body is maintained so that his clothes hang *'just so'*. He gets on with your friends without flirting with them, but they're in love with him anyway."

"Fuck." He lies back down on the bed, wholly intimidated. "I kind of feel like *I* want to date him." *That's normal.* Most men I knew were intimidated by my college boyfriend. My mum would have hated him. It doesn't do to date out of one's social status.

"Precisely. It was utterly exhausting."

He squints for a second. "Was he—?"

"You're going to waste a whole question asking if he was the one who proposed? Yes. He was the one who proposed. I don't talk about that."

"Got it." He cringed. "So I'm following him? Sucks to be me. Okay, then, my second—"

I hold up my fingers. "Third."

"Third question is, how are you going to describe me?"

"The one who got away."

He grins. "Ooh, I love that. I mean, I hate it, but it's a good choice."

"He's devilishly handsome, but not in a way that people are intimidated by it. He would have made a devoted husband and a loving father. He would have bought me gifts that I wanted on my birthday and Christmas, like a book or something cute that brings back a memory, then he'd have surprised me with a piece of jewelry that I didn't know I was getting. He'd have cried when he saw me walking down the aisle and every time I gave birth. We would have argued but never gone to sleep on an argument because we love each other so much. He would have kissed me every day like it was the first time, told me I was the most beautiful woman in the world and held my hand through all the tough times. But he's doing that for someone else, because the timing wasn't right. It wasn't meant to be, and it would never have worked. "

"Wow. Did you love him, though?"

I pause. Take a long, pensive breath. "Yes. Stupidly he's the only one I've ever loved. The men who follow him pale in comparison, but it's not their fault and I don't blame them. In fact, they never know. They can seduce me and take me all over the world, fulfill my wildest dreams, but they will never be him." He goes to reply but I put a finger over his mouth. "Last question. Use it very, very wisely. "

"So you were his first kiss, the first woman he dated and his first sexual partner, but he was your first love?"

"Yes." I choke on my reply, much more than when I'd actually used the L word. Tonight isn't about being miserable and sad because it's over. It is celebrating the little time we have. If I start crying, I won't stop. That's for tomorrow. Tomorrow will be work all day to forget then quilt hovel and Netflix all night for crying.

He holds me until dawn, neither one of us having slept. The conversation turns from love to music to books, to everything we could possibly want to know. He started it by saying that he didn't want to wake up in twenty years' time and wonder why he never knew more about me. Now he knows everything.

He never utters the L word or comments any more on the fact that I did. As we pack up our things and he takes me back to the truck, it is left unspoken.

Will I be wondering in twenty years' time if the one who got away loved me back?

"Give Mackenzie a chance," I say as I disembark from his truck the next morning. "If I'd never existed, would you have said yes?"

His lips twitch. "But you do."

"Promise me you'll think about it." I smile, grim but determined.

He shakes his head and I close the door. I hate myself for forcing the issue. I hate myself even more for coming into his life and messing with his mind. I could so easily have walked away.

He deserves to be happy — just not with me.

Chapter Seventeen

Eli

"Hi, this is Milly. Sing me a song or tell me you love me after the beep. *Beeep*." This is my third try. The little ditty she sings on her messaging service made me laugh at first, but now it just makes me sad.

"I was wrong," I say. "I should never have agreed to walk away. I can't do this. It's too hard."

"...tell me you love me after the beep. *Beeep*."

"I know you giggled when I said 'hard'. Call me back. Please."

"...love me after the beep. *Beeep*."

"Milly, you're the only woman for me. Your intentions are pure, I know that, but everybody is just waiting for me to ask Mackenzie to court me, and all I can think about is how much I want you and need you. Please don't do this."

Sometimes I feel like a raccoon, tracked by a coyote.

All I want to do is get on with my life, live it the best I can, but I'm trapped in a corner — and it's eat or get eaten.

I'm prey.

My parents told me that they've accepted my courtship with Mackenzie on my behalf. She's been over for tea a couple of times, and out of courtesy I took her to see my horses. She was right. She's a natural with them.

"…after the beep. *Beeep*."

"I just…everywhere reminds me of you. Everything I do, all my favorite places. I passed by the coffee shop today, but you weren't there. Stupid, I know, but I just wanted to see your smile."

I open the envelope in front of me. It's a card from Mackenzie, decorated with horses and hearts. I'm sure it's real pretty, if you like that kind of thing. The message inside reads, *'I know you're not ready. I don't even know if I am. We should at least try. Maybe we can make each other happy.'* She's such a sweet girl and it breaks my heart to think that she's being forced into this, too. My mama said I should take her out for a picnic. That's not the worst idea. It can't hurt to get to know her.

"…the beep. *Beeep*."

"I know I'm wasting my time but I can't walk away without at least trying one last time."

The picnic was nicer than I thought it would be. We talked about heartache. Mackenzie told me she was in love with someone, still thinks she is. I told her the same. In some way it brought us closer together. She wanted to hold my hand, so I let her. It was pleasant, not as wrong as it should have been. She asked me to try, so I agreed that I would.

My heart is broken.

"*Beeep.*"

"This is my last call. It was always you. It will always be you."

* * * *

Milly

Carrie, who has her treatment in a couple of days, has prepared a veritable feast for tonight. I can rest easier knowing that she is feeling well enough to cook and bake and that my life since I last saw Eli has been so busy that the only time I cry into my pillow is when I fall asleep at night.

I'm going to call this a win.

I should have walked away, never gotten involved. I reassured my conscience by making sure he would have no regrets, never realizing that I would be the one who regretted it the most. Turns out I *can* love after all.

In an attempt to drown my feelings, without the habitual break-up vodka binge, I've been attempting friendship. To be clear, I have friends back home, but I don't really do friendship as such. This has nothing to do with my traveling-free spirit, don't-get-attached theories that I attribute to relationships and everything to do with the fact that I am simply really bad at friendship.

And that I left school at sixteen and traveled around the world living out of hotels for three whole years. That makes it difficult to get attached.

I've been hanging out with the gang for two weeks now. I'm better than I ever was at crafts — which is both a mystery to me and hilarious to my aunties, who spend most of their time watching TV in bed since I gave them my Netflix password. I have gifted them with badly made bead bracelets, and in return, they have left me alone to wallow in my pity.

And wallowing I am, under my quilt with a good book and some refined sugar when a knock at the door disturbs me. I growl at the interruption, but nobody goes downstairs. The aunties are heavily invested in an episode of *The Crown*.

"Yes?" I say through the door.

"It's me...Eli." I open the door a crack. He's fiddling with his hands and kicking an invisible soccer ball.

"Hi." I run my fingers through my hair and find a popcorn kernel. This is not a good look. "You could have called to say you were coming."

"You don't answer my calls." *Touché.* "I brought you this."

He hands me an invitation with my name on it. It has metallic heart stickers and a blue and pink ribbon on the corner. I don't quite know how to process that.

He's on the verge of crying. "I...uh... We would really like it if you came." It's a punch to the gut. Not three short weeks after my last night with Eli, he is announcing his courtship with Mackenzie. I'd like to say I'm happy for them, but it would be an outright, bare-faced lie.

"Is this what you want?" He looks at me, his lips pursed, and gulps away the tears building in his eyes. He really doesn't want me to see him cry. "Eli, people who love you don't make you do things you don't want to do. You taught me that."

"It's not like I have a choice." Is that aimed at me or his parents?

I put the invitation in the pocket of my hoodie and step out onto the porch, taking his hands in mine.

They're warm, rough from looking after his horses and doing up his house. I turn them over and inspect them, run my thumbs over his palms as I search for my words. "You always have a choice."

"Not when it came to being with you."

I look up into those sad blue eyes. My lip trembles. *Damn it, Eli. I was getting over you.* "Don't make this harder than it is—because it is so fucking hard. And I'm doing my best and I need to be happy for you, because this is what was supposed to happen. I'm not what you need, and you know that. They will never accept me, and you will never leave. We'd be miserable."

"I am miserable."

I lean forward, he bends down and our foreheads touch. I want to kiss those lips so much that it physically hurts to stop myself from doing it. "No, Eli. If you've made the choice to be with Mackenzie, you have to be happy about it, for her." I can hear Sal descending the stairs. "You need to go."

"Goodbye, Milly." There's a thousand words being said in that one short sentence. This is my last chance to take him back before he is no longer mine.

Tell him how you feel, Milly. Kiss him, hug him, run away with him.

He turns, trundles back to his truck, his head down, a broken man. "You have a choice," I say. "It's not Gilead." But he doesn't look back.

Chapter Eighteen

Milly

There is one unspoken rule in Carrie and Sal's coffee shop. Harry and Susan don't pay. At first glance, Harry is a dapper old gentleman—always in his fancy suit, donning his favorite hat. But on closer inspection, his cuffs are frayed, his shoes held together with painted duct tape.

An iced tea or two and a piece of pie are worth it for his company when we set up in the morning. He regales us with a little song or his favorite story about the time some high-schoolers scaled the water tank and got stuck and other wildly exaggerated tales from the history of the town. Every time the stories get more fantastical, more incredible.

Susan, however, is a whole other story. She's married to a Booth. I've seen them at Sunday lunch. She gets two coffees a day, mostly just to have something in front of her so the other customers don't get suspicious.

We don't talk about the bruises or why she sits at a back table, hidden from the view of the window for a good part of every day. It's not for company, and she never talks. She just puffs on her electronic cigarette and smiles graciously when handed a coffee.

"Can I take that for you?" I'm clearing away the tables. She knows I'll get her another one.

"Thank you." The cut on her cheek needs stitches. At a guess, I'd say he caught her with his ring.

"Oh." The weight of the cup surprises me. "Are you not thirsty today? Did you want something else?" Come to think of it, she didn't drink the last one, either.

She glances up at me. This is more conversation in one minute than we've had in a month. "No, thank you. I don't like to be a bother."

"No bother at all. How about some of Carrie's sweet tea?"

"I... I don't know if I should." I sit in front of Susan, causing her to visibly recoil from my presence. Sal's eyes bore into the back of me. *We do not bother Susan.* Unspoken rule number two. She's so much younger than I first thought. Now we're face to face, and I can see she's around the same age as me.

I can do with punching someone myself right now, with all my rings on. He needs to try it with someone who will fight back.

"Susan, are you pregnant?" Her eyes widen in terror, but she does not reply. I pull my phone out of my pocket, look up women's shelters in Austin and leave it on the table in front of her.

The clattering echoes around the almost-empty café as I open the dishwasher drawer full of clean glasses. Sal is cleaning the coffee machine. "We don't bother Susan. You know this."

"The situation has changed," I mutter through my teeth.

"We don't want any trouble, Milly."

"I can't sit back and let it happen. I would never forgive myself if—" The jingle of the door signals a couple of last-minute customers, cutting the conversation dead.

My hometown is a small suburb in the southeast of England. Britain has a system of hierarchy unlike any other country. My town is majority working class. Unemployment is rife, as is crime. Coming from a broken home is not unusual, nor frowned upon. In fact, it is the norm.

My nan, Doris, on my dad's side, has been married four times. She likes to cheat, so she always picks men she doesn't love—drinkers, like her. We never went to my nan's when we were kids. Mum didn't trust whichever boyfriend was currently in residence. I remember one man who would give me pennies. Another would send me down the pub to buy him a take-out beer. I was nine years old.

It's easy to forget that Sal grew up in this home with a revolving door of unsuitable, violent men. She helps Susan because she sees herself in her. But Sal ran away in the end, as far as she could go. And she is waiting for Susan to do the same.

Susan is gone by the time I have served the last customer. My phone sits at the end of the counter. Curiosity gets the better of me. She's made a couple of calls.

My heart is lighter as we shut up shop and head on home.

Chapter Nineteen

Milly

When the day comes, it is with a heavy heart that I pull on one of my good-girl dresses and prepare to celebrate the happy couple.

If I close my eyes, I can still taste the feeling of his lips on mine, still smell the faintest odor of his deodorant mixed with supermarket cologne. Today, of all the days, I love him more than ever. Today I close a door, knowing that no window will open—not here, not until I'm somewhere else, far away from this town.

"I don't want to go," I say as I tease Sal's hair into a French plait. She's as bad as Carrie. I'm going to have to book them both into Kaylee's salon to sort their mops out.

"I know you like the boy, but nothing happened, so it's not like... Wait, nothing happened, right? "

A blush rises in my face, and I bite my lip.

"Nothing happened, *right, Milly*?" adds Carrie from her comfy bed palace.

"Doesn't matter now, does it?" I reply, avoiding their questions.

A tear rolls down my cheek. I haven't cried for four days, damn it.

"Milly...what did you do?" asks Sal, pulling her hair from my grasp as she turns to stare. Grabbing my hand, she yanks me over to the bed. "Family meeting." My heart sinks. Why couldn't I just shut my fucking mouth?

Because I'm weak, and I can't hold it in any longer. I tell them everything. Well, not everything. They don't need to know all the sordid details. They get the gist.

"So, let me great this straight," says Carrie. "You like the guy, but you know nothing's going to come of it, so you agree to a deal where you date him, teach him all about women then you split up. "

"Correct." I purse my lips, just like my mother. I'm not looking too great in this scenario.

"Except you went and fell in love with him because he's a Booth and that's what they do. They make you fall in love with them." Carrie closes her eyes, shakes her head. What must she think of me?

"He's not like the others."

She grins. "Oh really? So it doesn't bother you that a mere three weeks after you spend a passionate night with him, he announces his courtship?"

"Of course it bothers me. I...uh... I kind of made him do it." I throw myself back against the bedhead in despair and stuff a pillow over my face.

"You made the only man you've ever loved declare his intention to marry another woman."

"Yes." The reply is muffled by my new pillow hiding place.

"Milly, are you are out of your damn mind?"

"Yes."

She pulls off the pillow. "You are going to that party, and you are going to look fabulous so that he realizes what a fool he's been to ever let you go. "

It's not Eli's fault. He doesn't need to be punished by seeing me looking amazing. Nor Mackenzie… She has done nothing wrong. "It's not like that."

"The fuck it isn't. The minute you told that boy you loved him, he should have gone through hell and high water to keep you in his life."

"I pushed him away." I play them the messages I received every day for a week. He begged me every which way to reconsider. I never replied.

"Oh, honey, why would you do that?"

I look at my hands, nails bitten down to the quick. "For you, for him. I didn't want to get you guys in trouble, and I would have made a miserable wife, stuck in this town, with the worst in-laws in the history of the world."

They glance at each other. "I was wrong," says Carrie. "I should never have interfered in your love life. You're—"

"But what about Mark? He still wields the power in this town."

"Mark can go fuck himself. Honey, you're always so busy running away from love. Your parents aren't boring because they're married. They were always insufferably boring."

Sal taps her other half on the arm, jokingly. "Hey, that's my brother you're talking about."

Carrie throws her a look. "Sally Parker, your brother has always been as dull as hell, and you know it. Don't go on letting this poor girl equate marriage with purgatory. Look at us. We've had all kinds of adventures." She bends down under the bed and pulls out a dusty box, like last time, only this one contains postcards. "Every place we've visited. Look at all this." There has to be at least a hundred postcards in the box, if not more.

"Settling down doesn't mean that your body settles. It means that you settle your mind," says Carrie. "No more searching. I don't mean that this boy is the one. Lord, you're only twenty-one, but love isn't a prison sentence. It's a release. The freedom to start breathing again. Sweetheart, you need to stop holding your breath. You're choking yourself."

* * * *

There is no waltzing into the party, pie in hand, this time. Well, we brought a pie because Carrie said we had to take a pie, but Sal is holding it, not me. I'm just trying to get one foot in front of the other.

"Chin up." Sal winks at me.

I plaster a fake smile on my face. "How's this?" She says nothing, rolls her eyes and chuckles to herself.

The heat is secondary to everything today. The overwhelming blast of the scorching sun as I got out of the car didn't even faze me. My hair sticks to my skin, which burns under the torrid rays. I simply don't care.

My heartbeat increases with every step I take until I have to stop and breathe. *You can do this, Milly.* I've faced worse things in my life than this, right?

I stroll into the backyard, hoping that I can do that thing again, where I'm floating above my body, watching it hug and say 'hi' to everybody, void of emotion. Sadly, I'm feeling every second of this excruciating experience.

He's with his friends, joking around as usual, looking like a fucking dream, making it hurt even more. I guess I deserve that. He glances my way, catches my gaze just for a second, then blanks me. I deserve that, too.

The girls are all huddled around chatting. I wander over. "Hi, guys, what are you all talking about?" Raylyn shushes me and pulls me in to the huddle. Mackenzie, hidden from view, is crying so hard she's got the hiccups.

"Ooh, my God! What are you going to do?" Addison is stressed.

"What's going on?" I don't even know if I want to know the answer. Does she know? Did he tell her?

"Milly," she says, looking up at me and grasping both of my arms. *Crap. She knows, she knows. Shit, shit, shit.* "Can we go somewhere and talk? You can help me. You know about these things."

What do I know about what? *Ugh.* I hope this isn't a kissing thing. I don't want to give any advice to Mackenzie about kissing Eli.

"Shall we go somewhere quiet and have a chat?" *Uh, no?* This is not how I saw this afternoon going at all.

She wipes her tears, loops her arm through mine and we head for the only place I know where we can talk in private. To be accosted, only a few steps later, by the man himself.

"Mack…enzie, Milly. What are you doing?" He has the most terrified smile on his face I have ever seen.

I grit my teeth. "Mackenzie wanted to have a little chat with me, just girl talk. Nothing you have to worry about." Fuck, I hope he gets that this wasn't my idea. "She's going to tell me all her secrets, but I'm *not* going to tell her any of mine." I laugh, but the nervousness makes it loud, and I end up just making a choked *'ha'* noise.

Can someone please rescue me? Anyone? Nope. Cool.

He gets it, or at least I think he gets it. In any case, he lets us pass.

"Thank you, Milly, for doing this," she says as she climbs up next to me on the dryer. I'd hand her a Mountain Dew to calm her nerves, but it's not really her thing.

"No problem. So what's going on?" She starts to sob again. What am I supposed to do? I hand her a paper towel. "I can't help you if you don't tell me."

"Nobody can help me." *Oh wow, okay.* This might actually be something serious.

"Mackenzie, there's nothing so bad that we can't sort out. Trust me." Unless it's hiding a body, in which case you're going to need one of the senior Booths. They're much more likely to know the best burial sites in town.

"I'm pregnant." *Yeah. That's not good.* And yet, at the same time, go you, Mackenzie, you little shocker.

I lean in. "Who's the father?" *It can't be. Nope. Not possible.*

"You remember that party, the one you picked us up at?"

Oh fuck. A chill runs down my spine. Not him. *Ewww.* "Ye-es. Oh, Mackenzie, what did you do?" Or rather, *who* did you do?

"You have to promise not to tell."

"Mackenzie, it doesn't work like that." I take her into my arms. "You can't just make a baby go away." This is not that kind of place. "You have to take responsibility for it. Does the father know? Is he someone you dated, or at least someone you like?" Her face drops. *Oh fuck.* It's Kyle, isn't it? She's going to say Kyle.

"Kyle." *I win. Do I get a prize for guessing the biggest asshole in town?* "But he didn't force me. I wanted to. I've always been in love with Kyle." A little bit of bile rises up my throat. And here I was thinking he was the kind of guy only a mother could love.

I resist the temptation, strong as it is, to inform her that marrying the brother of the guy that knocked you up is not the greatest plan, and instead I concentrate on the first problem. Commiserating her on her break-up with the love of my life can wait. "Does he know?"

"He won't return my calls."

The door opens and Theresa walks in — popping in for a swig of the good stuff, apparently. She frowns at us then turns to go. "Wait." I look at Mackenzie. "She can help you. In fact, if anybody around here is going to help you, it's Theresa."

I've no idea where that came from. I'm even surprising myself by what's coming out of my mouth. Maybe her comment last time about a lifetime of dull sex stuck with me. Maybe, just maybe, she wants to do something good in her life.

The two women look at each other. Twenty-five or so years separate them, but they have a lot more in common than they think.

"You don't want to get married, huh? Elijah's a dreamer, but with a firm hand he'll come around to getting a real job." *Fuck you.* The polite grin stays frozen on my face, but I kind of want to kick her.

I purse my lips. "Not quite. Well, I don't know. Do you still want to marry Eli?" She shakes her head. *Thank you, God.* "No, it's more serious than that."

"I'm pregnant," she blurts out, weeping again.

"Well, shit. Come here, honey." For the second time since I met her, the softer side of this hard woman comes out. "You won't be the first, and you won't be the last. Who's the guilty party?"

Mackenzie is too pitiful to speak. She taps me on the arm. "You want *me* to tell her?" I ask. *No thank you, please.* "Uh…Kyle. It's Kyle. Mackenzie is in love with Kyle." This time I can't even manage to hide my disgust.

Theresa's face looks similar to how I imagine mine does. "Oh my word, you want to shake yourself out of that one, sugar. That boy is not settling down for nobody, and he's hardly a catch." Seeing the similarities between her oldest son and his father, I'm surprised by her honesty. Then again, I guess with age comes wisdom. "But he will not shirk his responsibilities."

Seeing that my work here is done, I leave them to talk. I'm not sure Mackenzie is going to find happiness, whatever the resolution to this, but I have a feeling that Theresa will help her out, nonetheless. My bet is on a hush payment and a quiet adoption, but I'm praying that somebody here remembers that it's no longer the nineteen-fifties and lets Mackenzie choose for herself. Like I said, three out of four Booth boys turned out okay. Their parents must have done something right.

The woman who walks out of that laundry room strides with the confidence of someone who has a chance at love. The bond that's broken between me and Eli hasn't been repaired, but the path to happiness is now clear. This isn't anything to do with me. I must have done something exceptional in a previous life to get this lucky.

Unfortunately, I'm walking out of the frying pan and into the fire.

Chapter Twenty

Milly

Susan's husband is here, drunk and fuming and heading for Aunt Sal.

"You fucking bitch, where's my wife?" His grubby finger digs into her bony chest as he steadies himself, sticking out his other hand for balance and letting out a large burp.

How dare you do that to my aunt? Creepy men scare me, but this drunken idiot just makes me mad.

Sal is taken by surprise. "I…uh…" She steps back, away from him. The people at the party do a wonderful impression of not noticing what's happening and yet, at exactly the same time, watching, fascinated by the spectacle.

"It's not her you want to talk to. It's me." He swings around, a snarl on his face as he takes in what I'm saying. "Come on then. What are you waiting for? Come poke your finger at me, and see how far that gets you." I'm from the southeast of England, and trust me... We don't often back down from a fight, especially one we can win.

The problem with this idiot is that he thinks all women are easy targets. "Where the fuck is my wife?"

I open up my hands as if in praise and beckon him to me. "The wife you punched so hard that your ring ripped open her cheek? That wife? She's gone. So far away that you are never going to hurt her again."

I have the attention of the whole party now. Eli steps forward, but his father sticks out his arm. He wants to know how this is going to play out. *Wanker.*

Cousin Booth lurches at me, his pointy finger going in all directions. How did he find enough alcohol in this place to get that drunk?

"Tell me where she is or you're going to be sorry."

He is laughable. "What are you going to do? Hit me? Come on then, you waste of space. Try and hit *this* girl." The time it takes him to pull back a punch, I already know where it's going. I could have ducked in slow motion, and he still would have missed. My kicking foot—which has been wanting to work its magic on several people since I got here—finally gets to play.

I trip the fucker up...spectacularly. He careens onto his back, and within seconds my foot hovers over his balls. *Should I? Of course I fucking should.* I just wish I'd worn heels. My sneaker slams down onto his baby makers. With any luck, this pathetic excuse for a man will never reproduce again.

"Get him," shouts a voice from the back. I'm pretty sure it's Raylyn.

"Let this be a lesson to you gentlemen," I say, looking up at the shocked crowd. "The women of this town will no longer tolerate wife-beaters, drunks and" —I turn and give Kyle my best *I-know-what-you-did* look—"assholes."

I know nothing is going to change. I know the Booths control this town—the *male* Booths. This isn't *Footloose*. Ain't nobody going to be dancing and drinking at this year's prom. Hopefully the new generation can change from within. As they take the place of their parents, they learn from their elders' mistakes.

My excitement at having beaten this man is short-lived. What do I do now? Do I leave? I am saved by an unforeseen force. A large drop of rain plops on the dusty ground, swiftly followed by another. Within seconds, rain batters down on to us and the party runs for cover.

"Sal," I say, as she grabs my hand, bringing me out of my shocked state and dragging me toward the car.

My adrenaline has peaked, and I can feel my rush coming down. I'm going to be shaking any minute. I don't want anybody to see me in that state, least of all the men in this town.

"Wait!" Eli runs up to me grabs my arm.

"Get inside. You'll catch your death." I sound like my mother.

"Are you okay?" He grips my arm, his thumb gently caressing me.

Mackenzie and Theresa come out of a side door, surprised by the rain. I look over his shoulder. "You should go."

He glances back but does not change his stance. "Not until you tell me you're okay."

I wrench my arm from his grip, shaking my head. What does he want me to say? Of course I'm not okay. A lightning crack breaks the tension. "Get inside," I reply, turning to walk away. I don't look back but run to the car where Sal is waiting for me. A final glance reveals him still standing there in the rain, soaked through to the skin, as am I.

"Holy shit." She drives us out of the car park. "That was incredible. Incredibly stupid, but fucking awesome."

"I am so mad with the men in this town. Mackenzie's pregnant."

Her jaw drops. "What? Not—"

"No, not Eli. Prepare yourself for this one... Kyle."

She shakes her head. "Booth boys, huh? What are you going to do?"

"Fight back." My laughter is tinged with fear. The shock of what I did is catching up with me. Sal hasn't said it, but she must be wondering what this means for me—and for her and Carrie.

"So, did you speak to him? That's why you came, right?" She winks at me. No fooling Auntie Sal.

"No."

"So if his truck was following us, would you want me to slow down and let you out or not?" *What? Oh my God.* My head spins around faster than a barn owl's. I don't think I can do this. Can I do this? I'm already a quivering wreck.

"Yes. Stop."

I step out into the rain. There's nobody else around, nobody to see. As if I care anymore.

"Do you want me to wait?"

I'm in no danger here. "No. Thanks, Sal. I'll see you later."

* * * *

Eli

I stand there in the rain as it washes my sins from me.

And by my sins I mean letting this beautiful, strong, incredible woman walk out of my life after she told me she loves me.

How could I be so wrong? How could I let my daddy influence me so much that I find myself at my fucking courtship party with a girl I've never kissed, that I don't even like very much?

I mean sure, she's nice enough.

But she's no Milly.

I turn to look at my family, huddled just inside the door, calling me into the house.

My mama, the queen of hypocrisy. She could have stepped in, could have said something. She hates all this and yet she lets it go on. Got to keep up appearances.

My daddy. *Fuck*. I hate him the most. The punch to the gut that he gave me when I stepped forward to help Milly still riles my belly.

"*Don't*," he'd whispered, throwing his fist into my stomach so hard and sending me flying back three feet into my friends — hard enough to hurt, hard enough to stop me in my tracks.

Yeah, I hate him the most.

I have to make a decision — right here, right now.

Up until this moment I'm the unboxed toothbrush. Never been used. They might think they know what I've done, have an idea that something happened with Milly, but they're not sure.

They're wishing as hell that it was just a kiss, maybe some first base fumbling.

I'm still 'pure'.

If I walk away, if I go after her, they're going to know it's more. My joke of a courtship will be finished. I'll have made a choice, and it won't go in my favor.

Who's to say she'll even have me?

I start to walk toward my truck, their voices in the background calling my name.

One second with her is worth a lifetime without them.

My choice is made.

Chapter Twenty-One

Milly

The truck pulls away, leaving me standing in the road, the rain lashing down on my skin. He drives up to me, and I climb up onto the little step on the driver's side, nose to nose with Eli.

"Get in. You'll catch your death." The raindrops run down my nose and drip onto his arm. "I needed to know that you're okay."

"I am now." I lean forward to kiss him but he backs away. "I guess I deserve that."

"No. I mean, no, it's not that I don't want to kiss you. It's just that you know I'm still officially in a courtship. I haven't told her it's over yet."

"Uh, no, you're not." *What the fuck? Does he not know?*

"Uh, yes, I am. Did you bang your head or something? You just came to my party."

I peel my sodden hair from my face, stare at him. "You haven't spoken to Mackenzie?"

"No, I followed you out of the party. You just got into a fight. I needed to know that you were okay."

How the hell am I the person who has to tell Eli that the girl he's in a courtship with is fucking his brother? Seriously. He giveth and he taketh away. This roller-coaster of emotions isn't finished with me yet.

"Take me to a burger place, because I am starving, and I have once again managed to go to one of your parties and not eat a bite. Then take me to your house. You're going to need to be sitting for this one, and you do *not* want to go back to that party."

I love that he just does it, without question. We drive back to town, with me sitting up for all to see. We buy food, in front of enough people that it will be around town in minutes, and we head to his house.

His phone rings, then it rings again. He hands it to me, and I switch it off. "Who was it?"

"I don't know. You've already gotten six or seven calls—Kyle, your mum, Mackenzie." I get a smirk on my face. I can't help it. The smile rides my mouth until I'm laughing. Belly laughing.

"What's so funny?"

Snort giggle. "Did you kiss Mackenzie?"

"No, she's not like that. I didn't want to, anyway. Why is that so funny? Why are you laughing?" He does *not* know where that mouth has been.

The stress relief from cracking up so much you're crying real tears is the best therapy. "Because it's so stupid, this whole situation. Oh my God. You're all lying…all of you. I have yet to meet anybody who is actually sticking to the so-called rules in this town. It's a fucking mess."

He draws up in front of the house, pulls on the handbrake then just glares at me.

"I'm sorry." I take a couple of deep breaths and fan myself. "It's not funny. It really isn't. Oh my word." I swallow it down. "Right. Look. Mackenzie isn't going to marry you because she is in love with somebody else. Ironic, when you think about the fact that you're marrying her because—"

But he's not in love with me. He never has been. Not once has he ever said he loved me, sent it to me in a message or in any way let me believe that that is the case.

"Who?"

The cringe is real. "Kyle."

He takes it in. Digests it, like sour milk in his coffee. "Okay."

"It gets worse." My giggles are back. Now it's just the nervousness. He glares at me. "I'm sorry." Deep breaths. "They slept together...and—"

"What?" He slams his hand on the steering wheel like it's Kyle's face. "He fucked her and he was happy to let me marry her, without telling me." *Ooh shit.* I hadn't been thinking of it like that. I was totally seeing it from her point of view, not from the traitorous brother side of things.

My giggles cease. He leans forward, tapping his head onto the steering wheel, and I rub his back until he calms down. Everything's gotten really serious, and I don't quite know what to do. He's supposed to be the one who calms my shit for me.

"And?"

"What? Sorry? What?" *I think I'd like to leave now. Check please.* Where's my coat?

"You said *'and'*."

I lean back against the window. Why is this truck so small and cramped?

Telling him about the baby fills me with dread. I hate confrontation. He must have had *some* feelings for Mackenzie to want to spend the rest of his life with her. He is not going to take this well. "Maybe we should go inside first."

"Just tell me, damn it!" The Booth boys are shouting at me today, and I don't like it. Dizziness overwhelms me, my ears ring as the blood drains from my face and I start to cry.

"I have had it with you people today. All I try to do is help people and all you do is shout at me or expect me to solve everybody's problems. Ever since I got to this town, I've been doing everything for everybody else and it's making me miserable." I throw his phone into his lap. "Ring her your damn self."

He wasn't expecting such an outburst, or at least that's what I can gather from the look on his face and the 'bob, bob' motions he's making with his mouth. I am not the person he should be taking this out on.

I shiver. The rain has ceased, but the temperature hasn't gone down a damned notch. I need to get out of these wet clothes.

I grab the door handle. Time to get out of Dodge. The heat hits my chilled skin as soon as the car door opens. I still haven't eaten anything. The spinning worsens, my legs give way and I vaguely feel myself fall to the ground as I pass out.

* * * *

"Milly." His voice is sweet and tender, lulling me awake. I open my eyes. "Shit, you scared me. Don't do that." He pulls me to his chest. We are on the porch. He carried me here. I should swoon more often.

"Burger," I whisper.

"What?"

"I'm *so* hungry." He laughs at me, then lifts me up and plants a kiss on my lips—nothing too passionate or sexual, just a loving peck to show me it's all okay. But I want more. I lift my hand to his neck, keeping his mouth on mine, and embrace him with everything I have.

No kiss is a wasted kiss when it's with Eli.

He nuzzles my nose. "How about you eat while I answer my phone. I have to know, Milly."

I climb out of his arms and dust myself off. Pain sears up my back. That going to bruise. "Don't tell them where you are."

Good Lord, can you imagine if the whole tribe followed us out here? I don't think I can take any more drama today, and besides, I have other plans

"Why? Because you think they're going to hunt me down and try to make me come back."

"No." I help him up from the dusty floor. "Because we're going to make love as soon as I've satiated my hunger."

"Are we now?" He raises an eyebrow, his interest piqued.

I grab the front of his shirt pull him toward me and lick my tongue ever so slowly across his lips. "Oh yeah. Hot, *hot*, sex. A ton of it. I am going to eat you up for dessert. I'm fed up with letting you save yourself for the right woman. I *am* the right woman."

"Are you sure the heat hasn't turned your brain. I should remind you that until I've had this phone call, I am still officially courting someone else." I would do anything for him to not make that call, but he is a man of his word. He should know the truth about Mackenzie from her, not from me. I've already said way too much. "And I have been telling you that you are the woman for me since I met you."

"You've never said you love me."

He chuckles. "Because I knew you would break my heart—and you did."

Damn it. Say the thing.

Phone in hand, he opens the house to let me in and sits out on his porch, in the shade, calling the woman he is supposed to fall in love with.

I surprise myself by not hanging around on the other side of the door trying to listen in. I am past caring about Mackenzie and her infatuation with Kyle. Once this is over and done with, he is going to be mine. I don't know for how long or in what capacity, but I know I love him and I want him in my life—and that's good enough for now.

* * * *

"It makes me so mad." Eli has been pacing around downstairs for fifteen minutes shouting into his phone. I'm surprised he's got any battery life left. "Yeah, well, fuck you." Hopefully he's talking to Kyle. I wouldn't like to think he'd speak to either his mum or Mackenzie that way.

The sound of footsteps stomping up the stairs signals that phone time is over. I guess my plan to make it all better with sexy times has probably gone to shit.

I've grabbed a classic from Eli's bookshelf—or at least the one that's in his bedroom. I'm doing my best to look like I was totally reading Charles Dickens and not listening to his private conversations *at all*. He sits on the edge of the bed, his head in his hands.

I once again rub his tensed-up back. My heart breaks for him. This is not how he saw his day going — or his life, for that matter. "Do you want to talk about it or just hug? I give great hugs." He spins around and snuggles up into my chest like a cute little puppy. The cowboy hat has been removed at some point downstairs, so I get to play with those tight blonde curls, pulling at them and letting them spring back into place.

"People suck."

"They do."

He looks up at me. "You don't suck."

"I do, a little. Remember when I told you I loved you then refused to see you and insisted you marry somebody else?" I smile at him. Sounds kind of mean when I put it like that.

"Nah, you did that because you love me, because you're incredible. I'm pretty sure you don't suck."

"Did she tell you?"

"Yeah." He furrows his brow. "Like, no remorse, not the tiniest bit of regret as she told me that she fucked my brother, is deeply in love with him and is having his baby. I mean, wow! She's not even close to the person I thought she was." I have to admit she had me fooled, too, but I guess we all have our secrets. I wasn't exactly truthful, either.

"You lied to her, too, though, right? I mean, yeah, what she did was way worse — what with the guy being your brother — but neither of you were honest with each other."

"No," he says, sitting up and looking at me. "That's the worst of it. I was honest. I told her I'd seen someone in the past, told her that I'd fallen in love but that it hadn't worked out and that it would take a long time for me to feel that way again. I was one-hundred-percent honest with that bitch."

He'd said *love*.

"Love?"

"How many times do I have to tell you, Milly? It was you. It was always you and it will *always* be you. I love you." He pops his finger behind the collar of my dress, runs it along my chest. "But I don't want to talk about her, not here with you."

"No?" I lean forward, pull on the rim of his damp jeans. "What do you want to talk about?"

"Reverse cowgirl?"

"Have you been on Google again?" That man, honestly.

"Maybe. I have so many questions about positions — spoons and dogs and wheelbarrows." He pushes me back onto the bed, hitches up my skirt and runs a solitary finger under the crotch of my panties, sending a shiver directly up my spine. "But how about we start off with a little revision?"

He hasn't forgotten a thing about what I taught him last time. He climbs over me as I lift my dress up and over my head, undoes his jeans and shimmies out of them. His very best shirt almost loses a button in the race to get naked.

I lie underneath him and he swoops his arm underneath me, gently clasping the base of my spine and lifting me to him. He lands his mouth on mine, the two of us eager to get this party started. I can feel his hard cock against me, ready. I'm so excited about this like it's my first time, too, if that makes any damn sense.

He places me back down and scoots to the bottom of the bed, his fingers and tongue ready and waiting to do what they do best. I close my eyes as his lips brush against my clit. He takes his time, mastering his craft. Everything I said, every reaction I made last time has been memorized. He knows what I like, and he plays me like a goddamn fiddle until I can hardly breathe. "Make me come..." I whisper, grasping onto the curls on his head with the very tips of my fingers.

The waves of my climax run through me, and a satisfied chuckle comes from between my legs. "It's moving," he mumbles under his breath as he lifts his head and smiles.

He leans over and pulls something from his jeans. Condoms. Why the hell does he have condoms? I try to hide it, but he catches the disappointment in my face. Was he planning to sleep with someone else tonight?

"Oh no. *No*, this is not what it looks like." He cringes. "You want to talk about irony? My brother gave me these as a courtship present."

I raise a brow. "Wow. Yeah. Imagine if he took his own advice?"

"If he took his own advice, I'd still be at that fucking party, announcing my courtship to someone who would be closing her eyes and thinking of my brother every time I made love to her."

"*Ewww.*" I make an involuntary heaving noise. "Sorry."

He opens the packet and inspects the contents. "Don't apologize. The more you're disgusted by my brother, the more I love you."

"Well then, you must love me a lot." I take the condom from his fingers and show him how to open it. His eyes widen as he looks at it, wondering how that tiny little round thing is going to get on his dick.

In the final love lesson I will ever give to Eli, I sit up and roll the condom down onto him, pinching the end and making sure it's on correctly.

He squints at it, bites his lip. This is his big moment. "Do you still want to? We don't have to..."

"Oh, I have always wanted to. You?" He nods, visibly nervous. This is such a huge moment. "It's going to be really quick and you won't have much time to think about anything, but that's okay. It takes a little practice, and I don't mind that at all."

He leans down over me, and I guide him in. His eyes widen enough to make me smile and he tries to move but I can see the excitement is mounting already. He kisses me, taking it really slowly, gasping into my mouth with pleasure at every thrust. His pleasure excites me. He could make me come if he touched me, but I'm afraid that that might be too much for him. This is his moment, and I'm literally just along for the ride.

As if he reads my mind, he stops moving. He sinks his hand down to my clit and gently swirls his finger around it. "Like this?" I nod. I didn't even have to ask. It takes me seconds to come, the smooth rhythm of him inside me, the thrill of our first time together. I moan with pleasure as my core tightens around him and his hand drops away as he comes, too, speeding up into me, thrusting hard, losing control.

His face contorts, his body stiffens and he lets out the most almighty roar, shocking himself at the ferocity of his orgasm. He looks down at me, his hair forming a mass of delicious, unruly curls. "Holy shit. That was fucking incredible. It was good for you, right? You came, didn't you? I think I felt you come, but I'm not sure. It was like really intense then I had to go faster because I was going to come."

I smile. "It was amazing. *You* were amazing." He kisses me again and again, until I can't take it anymore. "You need to pull out and dispose of the condom."

"Oh yeah, right. Yeah, shit." He does as he's told, and I show him what to do with it. He lies down beside me, his hand on my stomach. "It's not fair that you're the most beautiful, sweet, kind person I know, and yet, ever since I met you, everybody has wanted me to stay away from you. Such a crock of shit."

"If it's any consolation, I was told to stay away from you, too. As if only virgins and boys who aren't Booths are good people around here."

"Well, your aunties weren't wrong about the Booths, but everyone was definitely wrong about you. Even you were wrong about you."

"Who knew I had it in me to fall in love?"

"Me." He winks at me and pulls me into his chest. "You think you're *'not normal'*, but you're capable of falling in love, just like everybody else."

He's not wrong.

I was, though. People don't cement their feet to the floor. They stick to each other, and by each other. They bond. They connect. They join.

* * * *

Eli

For the second time in my life, I wake up next to Milly.

The sun bursts through the uncovered windows, adding heat to an already-sweaty situation.

I wrap my body around her, pull her to me. My cock is hard, as it always is when I wake, but this time it has purpose.

"I have to go," she mumbles. "I have to work — if I still have a job, if Carrie and Sal still have a business."

She's talking about my father. The wrath of Mark Booth knows no bounds. Milly humiliated his nephew yesterday then slept with his son. This will not go unpunished.

She told me about what happened between my daddy and Carrie, explaining why she couldn't commit to me before. My promise that nobody will suffer because of us being together feels less valid in the cold light of day.

My grip on her tightens. I need her to be okay.

She snuggles into me, her warm naked body allowing some respite from my worries. She is mine — for now, at least — and that has to count for something.

"Can't we just stay here forever?" I say. My voice is raspy, tired. We've been in this bed since yesterday afternoon, but very little of that was sleep. I'm pretty sure we covered all the different positions — as much as you can in one night.

"Wouldn't that be fun? You have to face your family, and I have to face mine. We're grown-ups, and we've got this."

"You don't believe a word you're saying."

"Nope." My gut wrenches at the idea of facing my family. This is not going to be a walk in the park. She rolls over and grabs my cock, running her fingers up to the tip, rendering me speechless. "But we don't have to do it *right* now."

Last night was all about me, all about her giving me the best time of my life. All she wanted to do was please me. I won't lie, I don't mind being pleased.

But it takes two to tango, and we've got one condom left. And I'm fixing to do some pleasing myself.

Half an hour later, we peel ourselves out of bed and head back home. I grip her hand tightly all the way.

I don't want to let go of her now that I've got her.

"Call me after work. I've got to do the horses and work on the house tonight, but I still want to see you."

I have a lot of explaining to do. And I still work for my daddy's company.

If they're planning to cast me out for my indiscretions with Milly, they'll have to fire me, too.

Chapter Twenty-Two

Milly

I open the door and head for the kitchen. Carrie is busy cooking something delicious smelling for breakfast, while Sal packs up the pies for the day. "Thought you might have built up an appetite," says Carrie with a wink.

Eww. No. Carrie's like a mother to me. "Carrie! I am starving. I don't think I even ate last night."

"Ooh, I bet you did," adds Sal. I shake my head and cringe at the both of them. They're ridiculous with their knowing looks and cheeky winks.

"You two need to get out more." I sit at the table, my hand propping my head up to keep me awake. Carrie serves me bacon and pancakes with eggs on the side. That woman is a saint. "So, what's the plan here? Do you think Mark and the rest of his family are going to come at us? A boycott, health regulations. Does he have the power to shut us down?" I need to know how bad this is going to be.

They share a look. "You know what?" says Sal, sitting beside me. "I'm kind of getting a little tired of living a life dictated by what Mark Booth decides. Let him try. If he succeeds, we'll sell and move on, and if he doesn't, well then that's all good, too."

"Sal tells me you kicked Susan's husband's ass yesterday."

I stifle a giggle. "More like his balls, but yes."

She hands me another pancake. "You're a good person, Milly Parker. Don't let anybody ever tell you different. You've got a good heart. If those idiot Booths want to come after us for yesterday or because of your boy, well then, let them. We're stronger than anything they can throw at us."

We finish breakfast and head for the shop. The effects of very little sleep are starting to hit me. It's going to be a long day. My body is tired, and my brain is mush. If they do boycott, at least I can have a nap.

"No Harry this morning," I lament. I didn't think he'd be swayed.

"He'll be here." Sal is stacking up the mugs and cups. "He always is."

The rush normally starts about seven-thirty, but today it's quieter than I've ever known it. Not a soul. *Shit.*

Then it happens. Customers, all the customers — regulars, new people, some from even out of town. All women — every generation combined, every woman I've met since I came to the place.

The place is so busy that Sal has to call in the other barista and rush off to get more pie.

"No more wife-beaters, no more drunks and no more assholes," says Raylyn, popping to the counter for a refill. "There was a rumor going around that some people might have decided for us that we shouldn't come here anymore." She leans right in and whispers, "Fuck them."

"Raylyn, you saucy minx, I love you."

"And here was me thinking someone else had stolen your heart — or is that just a rumor too?"

I shrug. "Meh, it might be." The grin on my face tells her everything she needs to know. Mackenzie's eyes bore into us from across the room. "But let's just keep that between us until the dust has settled, huh?"

She nods in agreement. "He deserves the best." Whoa, okay, controversial when we're talking about your best friend's ex, but I'll take it.

The crowd lulls as it always does in between the morning and the lunchtime surges. I tell the new barista, Carl, that he can go. There shouldn't be anything we can't handle from here on in.

He grabs his stuff and can't leave quick enough. Either he has places to go or he's heard I have a reputation for kicking where it hurts. As he's leaving, he holds the door open for a middle-aged woman. I know her from somewhere, but I can't quite place her.

"We're not expecting any deliveries today, are we?" says Sal, coming out from the back laden down with a stack of pies. "Ooh, it's quieter in here now, isn't it?"

Of course. She's the delivery woman. I remember her from my first day. I must have missed her every time since.

"I'm not working today. I'm here for Susan." Sal and I share a look. How can this woman be the only person who doesn't know what went down yesterday?

I take a sharp breath. "She hasn't been in for a few days."

"No, sorry. I mean I'm her aunt. I came here to thank you. We've all known... I mean, we all saw..." *And you did nothing?* "But she wouldn't let us help her. It broke my goddamn heart, it did. That poor girl. I don't know how you did it, but she's safe now. She wanted you to know, and she wanted to say thank you."

Sal puts down the pies and takes my hand. "It's thanks to Milly here. We care very deeply about Susan, but she wasn't ready until now. She always knew this place would be safe for her."

I'd always wondered why she came here, what enticed her to sit in here all day, but now it's clear. At some point, in some way, Sal or Carrie had made it clear that this was a safe place. My love for my aunt grows a little stronger, as if I didn't already adore her.

"Well, I just wanted you to know that she's well and that you'll be sure to get customers from every member of my family. What you did yesterday, Milly, was very brave, standing up to that man. We sure thank you for it."

She buys way too many coffees and a whole pie then leaves us to clear up the mess from this morning. I grab a tray and a cloth and head out into the shop, beaming from ear to ear with pride.

Community has always been a dirty word to me — people getting in your business, everybody knowing who's dating who. I was never a fan, especially when word got back to either of my parents about something I'd done. But it's growing on me. The kindness that has been bestowed upon me, a perfect stranger, ever since I got here is making me want to stick around.

No cement, no roots, but just a touch of glue. A piece of gum. Some double-sided sticky tape. Enough to hold me here a while longer

After I've cleaned up the tables, Sal lets me sit out the back for half an hour with a drink and a sandwich. I'm glad of the rest. It's been an awfully long day, and it's not even midday. I close my eyes and relive the glory of the previous night. Elijah Booth is my boyfriend and that makes my heart swell and my lady-parts flutter.

"Milly." Sal's voice wakes me from a deep X-rated dream and I found myself slumped over supply boxes, a little drool coming from the side of my mouth.

"Shit. How long was I asleep?"

"You were asleep?" *Oops. Busted.* "There's someone out here who wants to talk to you."

I run my fingers through my hair and try to adjust to reality. That dream was good.

"Actually, I'd like to speak to both of you, if I may?" says Theresa Booth. "I think we all agree that a little chat is in order."

There's not a customer in sight. I've missed the lunchtime rush, and Mondays aren't that busy anyway. Sal flips over the sign to read *'Closed'* and we grab a drink and sit around a table out of view of the window.

"Cream?" I ask, handing a black coffee to her. "Sugar?" She wants both and I grab some from the counter. She's nervous, shaky. Lord, don't let her husband have taken any of this out on her. She smiles as she takes a sip, probably wishing there was a dash of bourbon in it, too.

"Sal." She turns to my aunt, takes her hands. "I should really be addressing this to Carrie, but I don't want to bother her, with—you know—her being sick and all. My son told me what Mark did to her, how he treated her. I swear I had no idea he did that. It might have changed a lot of things in my life if I *had* known, probably wouldn't have my four sweet boys, so, you know, you have to think that these things all happen for a reason. Anyway, I'm so sorry for what he did." There's a sadness in her eyes today, more so than every other time I've been in close contact with her.

If things weren't so complicated, if I weren't dating her son, I'd tell her to leave him, that there's still time to make something of her life, but I can't save every damned woman in this town.

"Thank you, Theresa," says Sal. "You know, if you ever want to talk, I'm here, any time. You don't…well, you know, I'm always happy to help."

Theresa nods, graciously, and they share a conspiratorial look. Maybe I won't have to help her, after all. "And as for you, young lady, I hear you're courting my Elijah."

"Dating," I reply, "with no purpose."

She smiles, taking her hands from Sal's and placing them over mine. "Whatever you want to call it, you should know I'm very happy for you. He dodged a bullet with Mackenzie, and he just seems so in love with you."

My heart does a little leap. He *loves* me. He's my *boyfriend*. My mouth forms into the widest, stupidest grin, and I can't shake it.

"Thank you. Is…is Mackenzie okay?"

"Sure. Kyle has accepted all responsibility and…" She looks over at Sal, hesitant to discuss it in front of her.

"She knows. I should imagine everybody knows by now, in this town."

"Well, she's going to be okay. I've been talking to her folks, and we're going to get it sorted, however *she* wants." I fucking hope Mackenzie doesn't get it into her head to want to marry that man. It's out of my hands now, anyway. "Well, that's all I wanted to say. Milly, you are welcome in my home any time. Elijah has made it clear that he's moving into his house, so I guess you won't be over that much, but I wanted you to know that there are no hard feelings, despite our...differing opinions on how things are done over here." She gets up to go, hands me her empty cup and waits for me to stand before pulling me into the biggest hug. "Welcome to the family, Milly, if you'll have us."

Holy crap. She sure knows how to put the fear of God into a person who is afraid of commitment. I do my best not to shake my head and run for the hills. This is all a bit much, really.

Sal grabs my arm, as if she knows I want to bolt. "Do you have anything to say to Theresa, Milly?"

I grit my teeth. "I do. I'm sorry if I misled you or lied to you in regards to my relationship with Eli. Thank you for accepting me into your family." *And for not making everybody boycott the shop and for not having me thrown me out of town.*

Today's episode was brought to you by the word 'conciliation'.

* * * *

My ride home turns up half an hour early, way too eager to get me alone. "Hey, gorgeous."

"Hey, handsome."

He leans over the counter and pops a kiss on my lips. "I missed you today."

I giggle, stare into those baby blue eyes, and rub the tip of my nose against his. "It's only been a few hours." This man is all kinds of in love with me, and he is *glowing* — the glow of a man who sowed his oats last night. He needs to tone that shit down.

"Enough to miss you." He lands his lips on mine again. It is definitely time to get this man home.

He's kissing me...in public. And there isn't even a ring on my finger. *Scandalous.* I look around to see if anybody is watching, but nobody cares. I'm so disappointed. I want to show off my man and nobody cares.

"I hear you moved out."

"It was suggested that if I was going to start acting like an adult, I should live like one, too. The house is livable now, anyway — hot running water, a cooker and a bed. It's all we need."

"We?" He has the decency to blush. "Hot running water, huh? Who could turn that down?"

He throws on a fake smile. "Very funny. Are you ready to go? I need to talk to you about something. I have plans. Big plans."

I grab my bag and jacket and kiss my auntie goodbye, explaining that I might be late coming home tonight — or maybe not at all. "I need to pop home and get a change of clothes."

"No problem." He grabs my hand, like it's the most natural thing in the world. And yet it is.

I'm in a couple, like a real proper grown-up this-might-go-somewhere couple. Is this what it's like to be in love? That warm fuzzy feeling inside and the desperate desire to spend every waking hour in someone's presence.

It isn't what I expected at all.

Quite the contrary.
It's the most normal feeling in the world.

Epilogue

"Hey, you guys." My two favorite aunties, squished together so I can see them both, stare blankly into the phone at me.

"Is it working?" asks Carrie, peering into the camera. The question isn't aimed at me, but I answer anyway.

"Yes, I can see you guys. How are you?"

"Carrie got on the trial."

"Let me tell her. Milly, honey, I got on the trial." These two don't change.

"So I hear." Eli chuckles to himself, turns and winks at me. I whisper, "Eyes on the road, mister." He drops his hand onto my knee and gives it a squeeze.

We got the camper cheap and adapted it so that we could add a horse trailer behind. It took a few months of hard work, but that gave me enough time to help Sal set up a full-time barista so I could leave. There aren't enough days in a lifetime for me to get closer to Eli's dad, but his brothers and his mom accepted me with open arms. She had taken a good look at where her life was going after everything that had happened with Mackenzie and Kyle. She was working on things and, while he never talks about it, I know that meant a lot to Eli. He'd spent a lot of his childhood raising his brothers, and now he knew he could let go.

"Where are you?" asks Sal.

"Where are we, babe?" His mouth forms that cute little smile that he gets when I call him 'babe'. He doesn't think I've noticed — or maybe he doesn't even know he does it — but I see it every time. It makes my heart flutter to think that I love him and that he *feels* how much he's loved in everything I do.

"Bozeman, Montana — or we will be in about an hour or so." We've already been driving for several hours. Thank God we're nearly there. I'm starting to lose all feeling in my bum, and I'm exhausted after promising not to fall asleep this time.

"Hey, Eli!" the aunties sing in unison.

"Hey, Aunties," he replies.

"Look… I'll call you back when we get there, okay?" They hang up and I lean back in my seat. "I'm taking Smoky out when we get there. I need the exercise and so does he."

"Yes, ma'am."

We brought two horses along this time. Pepper is great for Eli's training sessions, but Smoky and I have a special connection. With two horses, I can join in the lessons. It's much more interesting than sitting on a fence, watching him do his thing. You can only do so much of that before utter boredom sets in.

It's so good to see Carrie looking so chipper. Her doctor gave her the all-clear a month ago. The drug trial will ensure — hopefully — that her cancer never comes back. Those two lovebirds deserve the world, and now it looks like they're going to get it.

I grab Eli's hand, which has climbed up my thigh and is dangerously close to inciting me to make him pull over. I kiss the back of it then place it back on my thigh, still clasped to mine.

An overwhelming love fills me.

Look at us, on the open road, doing our thing. He's been holding training sessions for colts for a couple of months now, and he's getting so good at it. Of course, it helps that he absolutely adores both the horses and the job.

This is exactly how I saw my life, traveling, meeting new people. I didn't imagine for a second that it'd be possible to do it with someone else — and even less with Eli.

But we did it. We made our own rules, chose our own path, and that's what makes it work.

"Pull over," I say, squeezing his hand even tighter.

"But...Milly." He shakes his head in fake desperation, a wide grin on his face. "We're almost there."

"Just ten minutes."

"Twenty," he replies, clearly affronted by my lack of faith in his abilities. "Thirty, if you let me find out what a sixty-nine is."

Good God. I'm banning that man from Google.

"Deal."

Want to see more from this author? Here's a taster for you to enjoy!

Mixed Emotions: (Mis)Taken
Katy Hunter

Coming July 2022

Excerpt

Penny, you're a strong, capable woman. You will not falter at the sight of an exposed ab, a kissable lip or a murmured 'I love you'. You've got this. You can do it.

I raise a trembling hand to knock, hesitating before going in for the kill.

To be entirely truthful, I don't have 'it' at all. In fact, I'm about as far from having 'it' as a person can be, but Kelli's eyes are burning a hole in my back as she stares me down from her car—willing me to do the right thing—and I don't want to get my proverbial arse kicked if I fuck this up.

To my surprise, the front door opens. The decision is made for me. "Hey, Penny."

"Hey." Reece's stunning older sister Chloe brushes past me, giving me a quick peck on the cheek and leaving the door wide open. Her manner is such that I'm pretty sure she has no idea why I'm here or what her brother has been up to. This doesn't shock me. The man is sly. He's not going to let the world—or his family—know that he fucked up another relationship.

"Reeeece, Penny's here," she yells over her shoulder as she leaves.

Would he have answered if he hadn't been forced to? It's been two weeks and the man has completely ignored my calls and been suspiciously absent every time I come by. *The Art of Ghosting* by Reece Sheffield. It wouldn't sell well, the proof being that I'm standing on his doorstep right now listening to him come down the stairs.

A conversation is well overdue, and now he can't avoid it. *Good.* At least it'll be over with.

He saunters down the corridor. Reece's at-home attire is a pair of gray tracksuit bottoms. He's been wearing them for so long that the crotch has started to thin and the elastic in the waist has gone to shit. He never wears anything underneath them, so I—and possibly all his neighbors—am treated to more than just an impression of his family jewels.

He scratches the back of his neck then rubs it. Too much late-night gaming again. Not my problem anymore.

Then he slips his hand into his pocket and scratches his junk.

Don't look at his penis. I allow my eyes to drop down, just for a second. I can see why Kelli felt like I needed back-up for this mission. I am confoundedly drawn to the enemy.

He has bags under his eyes and the imprint of his pillow on his cheek, but he's still devastatingly handsome. Even his hair is flattened on one side, which should be wholly unattractive and yet, *God…* I want to run my fingers through it, pull at it, hold it while he…

Kelli's voice seeps into my mind. *"Don't fall for him again. I'm warning you. I won't be afraid to get out of this* car and tell him exactly what I think of him. It won't be pretty, Pen."

"Hey," he says, flashing me a subtle smile and leaning into the doorway. "You want to come in?"

Yes, please. Damn it. No. Be strong. Ignore the dimples. Move away from those come-to-bed eyes.

"Nah. I'll just make this quick, shall I? It's over. As if it could be anything else after what you've done. I'll get someone to drop your stuff off, and if you could do the same, then we can close the chapter on this whole thing."

"Pen..." He takes his hand out of his pocket and scratches his abs, revealing just a glimpse of the little hairline that runs up his stomach. I used to kiss that, on my way down. That might be the bit of him I'll miss the most. "Don't be like that."

"Don't be like that?" What the fuck? Tomorrow was supposed to have been our wedding day.

"We haven't spoken in two weeks. We were getting married, buying a flat, growing old together. Remember that?"

"Yeah..." He contorts his face into the most unpleasant grimace, like I've just suggested that he clean the skid marks off the toilet. "No. I can't do that anymore."

He's so casual, almost emotionless...as if he's canceling a lunch date.

"I figured that when you ran away the other day, *during sex*, and haven't spoken to me since."

It had been *terrible* sex. Neither of us had been in the mood. We'd been arguing the finer details of our quickie registry office wedding, and all I'd wanted was the final say on the flowers. I *may* have asked him about petunias as he pounded away aimlessly. It wasn't my finest moment, and if it's any consolation, I do regret it, but still, I'm not sure it quite merited *this*.

"Yeah." I've never noticed how monosyllabic he is until now. "Sorry."

I cackle. "Sorry? Are you sorry for cheating, too?"

This one throws him. When he isn't half-asleep in his manky old clothes, Reece is on everybody's TV from nine a.m. until lunchtime. Suited and booted, he climbs into a company car every day — an air of complete confidence — and heads off to convince everybody that he is the perfect gent. Witty, handsome, caring... He has the whole country fooled into thinking he's such a fucking catch. That was the man I'd fallen in love with, and that is the man who is about to emerge onto the doorstep at the realization that *I* am dumping *him*.

This isn't me begging him to come back. This is me telling him he can fuck right off. From the look of the storm brewing in his eyes, he is *not* happy about it.

He narrows his eyes. "I didn't cheat on you, Pen. I walked out on you two weeks ago and found myself someone who wasn't so desperate to get married and have babies and all that shit — someone who pays attention when I'm fucking her."

"We were *engaged*, Reece. Nobody forced you into proposing."

"You haven't talked about anything else since you met me. You keep bridal magazines on your coffee table. You decided where we were going to live, our kids' names and you even chose a fucking puppy at the shelter." I step back. His voice has a tinge of menace, and confrontation isn't my thing. I wouldn't have come here today, but Kelli made me.

"*That's what best friends are for,*" she'd said as she'd dropped me off at the end of the road. "*Now go dump that idiot.*"

She has never liked the man. Now I'm starting to come across to her point of view. What had I been thinking? Perhaps, more specifically, which part of my body had I been thinking with? The man is a dream. Even a grungy T-shirt and skanky old trousers can't hide that.

Reece unfurls his hand from his neck and places it on my reddened cheek, pulling me closer. "You're angry with me. I get it. I *am* sorry." He leans in closer. "You sure you don't want to come in and let me make it up to you? One last time."

He smells like sleep and sweat and the aftershave I bought him for Christmas — and familiarity. I close my eyes, exulting in that delicious scent.

How amazing it used to feel when he held me so tightly that I thought he'd never let go.

How loved I was.

He brushes his lips against mine and a car horn honks loudly, making us both jump. Reece looks over my shoulder, trying to see who's out there.

"I can't do this. It's over." I hold out my hand. "Here's the ring. Thanks for the memories. Enjoy your incredible new girlfriend who doesn't mind the fact that nine times out of ten you're too tired for foreplay." Reece being 'not really into' going down on me had been somewhat of a relief. The man was terrible at it. He thinks the clit is to be treated like a button on a PlayStation handset, flicked relentlessly. He doesn't do subtle. He does quick and to the point. If lady-parts could curl up in horror, I'm pretty sure mine had just done that at the thought of being in this man's hands again.

He pushes my palm away, the ring still in it. "You won't find anyone like me."

I fucking hope not.

"I have options. So many options," I reply, with an air of self-confidence that's fooling nobody. I don't have a single option…not one. He leans his head to one side, contemplating the fact that somebody might be interested in me. My phone rings. 'Cute Coffee Shop Guy' is calling me, apparently. "Hello?"

Before I can stop him, Reece leans forward and puts the call on speaker. *What the fuck?*

"Hey, Penny, it's Jake. We met at the coffee shop the other day. You gave me your number for a gig."

"Hi, Jake." I know that voice, but can't quite place it. "What can I do for you?" Reece steps back into the door-well. I lift a hand, as if to wave goodbye, and back away a couple of feet.

"Look. I know you said you have a boyfriend, but, fuck it, I just wanted to say that if you're ever free…"

I glance back up at Reece, shrug my shoulders and smile. "I'm free tonight."

"You are?"

"Sure. Hold on a second. I'll just finish what I'm doing, and we'll work out the details." I stroll back over to a shocked Reece, lean in and peck him on the cheek. "So. Many. Options."

I lift the phone to my ear and chat away as I walk back down the street to Kelli's car, not even bothering to take him off speaker. This is a glorious moment and I want everybody to enjoy it, Reece especially.

I also slide the very expensive diamond ring back onto my finger. *Hell, I deserve it.* I washed that man's dirty underwear while he was sleeping with someone else. I should have married him *then* left his sorry arse.

"You killed it," she cries, hugging me as I slide into the passenger seat. "I knew you could do it."

I point at the phone. "*Jake?* Really? I thought Reece was going to twig."

She winks at me. "What is the point of me having the most *adorable* cousins if I can't use them to get back at that cheating dickhead of an ex-fiancé of yours?"

I grin. "True. Did you see his face? Oh my God. And I almost kissed him. Ugh. I'm so pathetic."

"You are," she replies, starting up the engine. "But I love you anyway. Now, how about we stock up on tequila and ice cream. In a couple of hours, you're going to remember that tomorrow was supposed to be your wedding day and you're going to be a mess."

"I'm fine." I'm on a high. Nothing can top the look on that man's face and the way I'm feeling right now. Kelli purses her lips. She knows me far too well. I'll be a sobbing wreck in a couple of hours and only margaritas can heal that type of pain.

* * * *

Kelli hands me a cocktail, which is deceptively orange, considering it's ninety-five percent alcohol. "He's a dick."

"No, it's my fault. I did it again."

"You did nothing wrong." She takes my hand. "Nobody forced him to put that ring on your finger."

"True." But I'd been sowing the seeds since we'd met. Marriage, babies, a home, that's the goal. That's always the goal and always the problem. Sometimes I let that goal spill out from my internal thoughts to my external ones. "I think I gaslighted him into proposing. I'm very persuasive."

"Fuck off. You should have given him a kick where it hurts. What a tosser, running off mid-sex. I can't believe it." She downs her cocktail, inciting me to do the same, then pours us another. "I mean, who makes someone move to another city, proposes to them then

just fucks off, you know, while they're fucking. *Fucker*."
Kelli is not one to mince her words.

"Can we change the subject?" I'd rather talk about anything than that man. I can't stop thinking about that hand running across those abs and how I'll never see or touch them again. I was right. I *will* miss that delicious line of hair the most.

"We sure can. You know what this night needs?" She pulls out a folder from under the coffee table, but it's not just any folder. It's a big pink four-clip wedding file covered in cut-out pictures from old teen magazines. "Perfect Husband Dan Scott."

Oh my God. I can't believe she kept that thing. We must have made it when we were fourteen. "Not Fucking Perfect Husband Dan Scott."

"Perfect Husband Dan wouldn't pull out and run. He'd smother the bed in rose petals then he'd smother your body with his until you couldn't take it anymore."

I grab the folder, open it to a random page. "True. And puppies… He'd get me a puppy. No, two puppies. No, he'd adopt *all* the puppies from the shelter."

"Yeah, he would. That's more like it. Then he'd invite you back to his beach house for romantic walks on the sand at sunset." *Oh, the dream*. Holding hands as we stroll along the beach. No need for words, as we know we love each other with a glance and a smile.

"Exactly. Yes. Can I have another one of your delicious cocktails?" Kelli serves me another drink and I turn the page. A photo from some random wedding shoot Dan did for a movie with my head glued on in the place of the bride stares back at me. It's like something out of a serial killer's lair. "Fuck, that's a bit warped."

Kelli peeps over my shoulder "Yeah, I think we went too far with that one."

Before it made it into the folder, that picture used to be on my wall. Before I even knew Dan, he was by my side being the perfect husband, waiting for me to grow up and marry him for real.

Dan might not really be the man of my dreams — that's just a joke that Kelli likes to perpetuate — but I love him very much. In fact, not a week goes by that I don't send him a 'Hi, how are you doing?' via our secret little WhatsApp group. He always replies something rock-and-roll like 'wasted' or 'chilling'. It's our thing and we've done it for five years now without a single person knowing about it.

He's more Secret Best Friend Dan Scott, but she doesn't need to know about that. I keep that for me.

The souvenirs that Kelli and I created to distract us from the torn shreds of our lives are just a silly game, but that folder reminds me of the actual dream — the one I keep in my heart, the one where I fall in love forever.

Perfect Husband *Somebody* has to exist, doesn't he?

About the Author

Katy Hunter lives on a mountain in France with her husband, kids and two dogs.

When she's not writing you can find her curled up in front of the fire, book in one hand and a glass of chardonnay in the other.

Katy loves to hear from readers. You can find her contact information, website details and author profile page at https://www.totallybound.com

Home of Erotic Romance

Sign up for our newsletter and find out about all our romance book releases, eBook sales and promotions, sneak peeks and FREE romance books!

www.ingramcontent.com/pod-product-compliance
Lightning Source LLC
Chambersburg PA
CBHW020418180626
46812CB00003B/1031